Pure Justice

No Escape, Paid in Blood

Linda L. Barton

Inspired by
Bob G. Barton

ISBN: 9780615968742

Dedication and Special Acknowledgement

To my wonderful husband, Bob.
You are the true creative force
in this writing adventure.
For it's your creative mind,
where our stories are born.

Cover Design and Formatting by
Deadly Reads Author Services

Chapter 1

Lisa was glad the day was finally over. The art show had been a complete success, and after standing all day, her feet were killing her. The new artist's work was bold and exciting; for this reason, there had been a large turnout with several influential people in attendance.

He's going to be quite famous in no time at all, she thought to herself.

Her boss had asked her to stay and clean up, so she would not be home until around 9 o'clock.

"I can't believe he left me here to do it all by myself again. I need to get a better job because this one doesn't pay enough to put up with his crap!"

Lisa never liked to stay at work after dark. The employee parking was in the alley behind the building, and the lighting had not worked since she started a year and a half ago. She had asked several times if they could get it working properly, but her boss would only tease her about being afraid of the dark.

"Come on, Miss Mathews, what's the problem? This is a nice part of town, so nothing will happen to you here."

She hated the way he made her feel. "I have a Masters Degree for God's sake! I can go to any place and get a better job than this!"

Lisa had taken the job straight out of college. Mr. Levtin was one of the leading art dealers in the country, so when the opportunity arose to work with him, she had jumped at it.

Lisa had always dreamed of submerging herself in the world of classical art, so when introduced to him at an art show during her final year, she knew he would be her ticket.

"Yeah, some deal this turned out to be. I ended up being nothing more than a glorified maid," she said aloud as she put the last of the champagne glasses in the packing box.

Next, she locked the door to Mr. Levtin's office, turned off the lights in the restroom, and then looked around the gallery one last time, making sure that everything was in its proper place.

"Okay, it's time to get the hell out of here," she sighed as she walked to the back door.

***

The man in the shadows was pleased that he had decided to wait.

This is gonna be easier than I thought, he said to himself silently.

He was relieved when the older man left a couple of hours earlier, leaving the young woman alone. He knew she would be an easy mark.

He had watched as the people arrived earlier in their long, black limousines, dressed in their expensive clothes, each wanting to be the first to see the work of the new, exciting artist.

Man, this place must be loaded with money. All those fancy people buying them stupid-looking statues. This place is a goldmine and will set me up for a long time; he smiled.

He never understood why anyone would pay thousands of dollars for art. *Damn fools, why don't you save yourselves some money and just buy a good porn magazine. Now that is art!* He chuckled.

"It's time, sweetie," he whispered to himself as he watched her come out of the back door. He waited for her to turn around to lock the door before making his move.

"Okay, let's have us some fun," he chuckled silently to himself.

The attack caught Lisa completely by surprise, as he slammed her against the door.

"Open the door!" he growled in her ear.

"Please, don't…" Lisa whimpered.

"Open the door, NOW!" He shoved her again, causing her to drop the keys.

"I can't…the keys! Oh, God, please don't hurt me! Take my purse; there's money in it! Please…, don't hurt me!"

Lisa knew the last thing she needed was for him take her back inside away from help. Her mind spun wildly when suddenly, a horrifying thought came to her. *He's going to rape me!*

"Please just take my purse and leave me. I promise that I won't tell anyone…please!"

It was all taking too long, and he knew the longer they were outside, the more chance there was of someone seeing them.

"Come on, bitch, I don't want your purse. Pick up the damn keys and unlock the fucking door!" He shoved her down toward the keys while still grasping her right arm. "Pick up the keys, NOW!"

Lisa knew if he got the door unlocked, it was over for her. She closed her eyes, searching her mind for what to do when it finally came to her. Last year a friend had convinced her to go to a self-defense class with her. Lisa was not interested at first but had finally gone along to make her friend happy. The instructor of the class had shown them the safest way to escape an attack. He had said to use anything you could to distract the attacker and then make your escape.

Lisa remembered the instructor saying how you could use keys as a weapon to distract your attacker.

Okay, here goes. She steadied herself then reached for the keys, firmly clutching them between her fingers.

"Hold on, hold on... I have them," she cried while trying to appear calm. She held her breath, stood, and then whirled around to face him.

The attacker did not have time to react before the keys raked across his face, and the pain was instant, causing him to howl in protest.

"You bitch...I'm gonna rip your fucking head off!" He grabbed her throat and began to choke the life out of her.

"I'm gonna enjoy watching you die, bitch!" he growled, seeing the terror in her eyes.

Lisa could not believe what was happening. *I'm going to die, and there's nothing I can do to save myself,* the words screamed in her mind.

The world around her began to grow faint, and a feeling of lightness moved over her body.

So, this is what it is like to die? She thought to herself as she felt her soul begin to slip from her body.

In her mind, she heard crying and then, to her horror, realized it was her own voice begging for mercy. Finally, realizing there was no escape from her nightmare, she closed her eyes and waited for the sweet release of death until something changed.

The death grip on her throat suddenly released. *What now, has he changed his mind?*

Standing with her eyes tightly closed and not sure of what to do, Lisa knew she had to act before he decided to attack her again. She swallowed and slowly opened her eyes. However, the vision that appeared before her was unthinkable.

His head is gone! Fear once again gripped her body, as she realized she could not move; she could not scream.

Lisa watched in horror as the headless body of her attacker crumbled to the ground. Her heart was pounding in her chest, and she wanted to run only; she found her feet would not move. Noticing something wet on her face, she reached up with a shaky hand to wipe away the offending substance.

She held out her hand. *Blood? Oh, my God, it's blood*! The words screamed in her mind as she felt the world closing in on her again. Her head was spinning as she fought to comprehend the vision before her.

Then as she began to slip into the darkness once again, a face appeared before her with cold, steel-blue eyes.

"Oh, God, please, no!" the words barely escaped her lips.

"Don't worry, you're safe now. He won't be able to hurt anyone again."

She barely heard the words, as his hands reached out to steady her.

"He has received what he deserved; justice is fulfilled."

His steel-blue eyes burned into hers with such intensity that she believed they would consume her soul. However, to her surprise, fear consuming her moments before now had vanished. Her eyes locked onto his like a lifeline, but what he did next surprised her. He smiled, pointing a gloved finger at his eye, and then down to the head lying next to the crumpled, bloodied body and softly said, "An eye for an eye."

Lisa's mind spun, trying to understand everything that had just happened, but the overpowering emotions surging through her body caused her legs to crumble beneath her. She felt the darkness flooding her mind as she looked into his eyes.

"Thank you for saving me," was the only words she whispered until she finally surrendered to the gentle arms of unconsciousness.

***

The media had a field day with the story of the woman saved by a mysterious vigilante. They loved that sort of story because sex and murder always made for a great headline. Lisa had answered every question the police asked when they came to the hospital, and she did not understand why they insisted on asking the same questions repeatedly.

"I don't know who he was. I've never seen him before, and besides, I only saw his eyes. They were a deep steel-blue." She knew she ought to have told them more, but, to be honest, she did not want to.

"Don't you all understand that he saved my life? I hate to think of what would've happened to me if he hadn't shown up when he did." She trembled at the memory of those cold hands closing around her throat.

"That guy said he was going to kill me. He said he was going to rip my head off! I'm alive because a stranger came to save me like an angel from heaven. I'm sorry, but you're going to have to find him on your own. I've told you everything I can remember."

When her story leaked out to the press, they ran with it like wildfire, and it was the lead story from coast to coast.

ANGEL OF DEATH SAVES WOMAN; DECAPITATES HER ATTACKER

Chapter 2

Thirty-Seven Years Earlier

"Get your lazy ass out of bed!" Mack and Terry were up and ready to go out for some fun in San Francisco before heading back to their homes and lives.

Mack reached down and jiggled Ted's bed. "Come on, Ted. Let's go see what kind of trouble we can get ourselves into today. We made it back to the world, so let's go enjoy it!"

Ted was tired. It was the first time in nearly a year that he had been able to relax. The last three months had been unusually rough, and it surprised him how the three of them had made it back alive from their tour in Vietnam. "Man, you two go on without me. I'll catch up with you later."

"Are you sure, man? Come on, you know that me and Terry won't get any of the sexy girls if you're not there for bait. The girls always swarm around you like bees to clover," Mack laughed, as he elbowed Terry.

"Yeah, and they take one look at our ugly mugs and run the other direction," Terry grinned, kicking the side of the bed. "You can't send us out there unarmed, man."

Ted grabbed the blanket and pulled it up around his neck. "You two can handle yourselves just fine without me. I'm happy right here. I'm going to enjoy this comfortable bed and being able to sleep without fighting off snakes or dodging bullets. If you guys want, we can meet at that Fisherman's Wharf we saw yesterday for lunch. Some steamed crab would be great with some freshly baked sourdough bread. How does that sound?"

Mack and Terry knew there was no sense trying to change Ted's mind. "All right, I guess we'll just have to do it on our own then. We'll see you around 1300 for lunch." Mack looked at Ted, hoping he might change his mind, but when he did not move, they both turned and walked toward the door.

"See you later…, sleeping beauty," Terry laughed as he opened the door and held it for Mack. The two of them turned to look at Ted one last time before they stepped through the door and closed it behind them.

"Finally, peace and quiet," Ted sighed. However, he could not help snickering as he heard Mack and Terry laughing and joking while they walked down the hall.

Those two are nuts; Ted thought to himself as he rolled over on his side and settled into a comfortable position. He closed his eyes, and a few minutes later, he blissfully fell back to sleep.

***

Ted Braxton was with 1st Marine Recon. He had always wanted to be a soldier like his father before him and was proud the day he enlisted. Since the war in Vietnam was escalating, Ted decided to enlist before they had the chance to draft him. His father had served in the Navy, but Ted wanted to be a Marine.

"Dad, you know I don't like the water that much," he would always say.

His father had served during WWII in the Pacific, so Ted had grown up hearing stories of his days at sea fighting the Japanese.

"Son, the proudest day of my time serving in the Navy was when I knocked that damn zero out of the sky. They were swarming around us like flies, trying their damnedest to send us to a watery grave, but he made a fatal mistake and got right in my sights. I blew the tail right off that plane!"

His father loved telling this story; his eyes would light up, and he would press his chest out with pride every time.

"Yep, I sent that little bastard straight to hell." He would laugh and slap his hand on his knee at the memory of that day.

After the war, his dad left the Navy and returned to Southeast Texas. He then married his childhood sweetheart and began driving a truck hauling trees to the mill. His parents had lived a simple life. For their first anniversary, they had celebrated with the birth of Ted, and then three years later, his brother, Jason, was born.

Ted clearly remembered how happy his parents were the day his mother found out she was pregnant for the third time. His mother told them how she had prayed for a little girl, and she knew God would give her one this time.

Of course, Ted and his brother sneered at the idea of a little sister. "Mom, why do you want a girl? Heck, the only thing they're good for is picking on and making them cry." They both said whenever she spoke of her desire for a daughter.

However, their mother would only smile and say, "You boys may believe that now, but once she's here, you'll think differently."

***

The last four months of the pregnancy were difficult for Ted's mother. Whenever she would try to stand for very long, she would get dizzy and nearly faint. Much to her distress, her doctor finally had to put her on complete bed rest.

Ted and Jason did their best to help their mother as much as two young boys could by keeping up with the house cleaning and laundry. They had worked hard so their mother would not get out of bed to do it herself. Then once their father came home from work each evening, the three of them would cook dinner and bring it into the bedroom so they could eat together as a family.

***

The night his mother went into labor was an unusually stormy one. The rain came down in sheets with lightning, and thunder filled the sky.

Ted would never forget the look on his father's face when they left for the hospital. Ted knew something was terribly wrong when he saw the blood on the floor, and the ashen look on his mother's face.

"Dad, is Mom going to be all right?" Ted quietly asked his father, as they helped her to the door.

"Son, she'll be just fine. You stay here with your brother and watch him. I'll call you once the baby gets here, and remember to keep the door locked. You're the man of the house until I get home." His father looked at Ted and gave him a reassuring wink.

It turned out to be the longest night in Ted's young life. He had sat watching the clock, convinced the minute hand was moving slower than usual. Jason had fallen asleep on the sofa about thirty minutes after his parents left, so Ted was alone with his imagination working up all sorts of terrible things. After a couple of hours, he finally slipped off into a restless sleep.

***

The sound of the front door closing startled Ted awake.

"Who is there?" he asked in a shaky voice, but as he looked toward the front door, he saw the ghostly looking figure of his father standing there.

"Dad, what's wrong? Where's Mom and the baby?"

His father did not respond; he only stood there with tears streaming down his cheeks. Ted had never seen his father cry; he had always been such a strong man in any situation. "Son, wake up, your brother; we need to talk."

The next several minutes were like a terrible dream. Ted could remember his father saying something about, *Too much blood, and they couldn't stop the bleeding.*

Jason began to cry, "Go get her daddy. You can't leave her at the hospital. She'll miss us. She'll be lonely without us!"

"I'm so sorry, son, but she is not coming home. Mommy and your little sister are in heaven. They're angels now and watching over us. Mommy didn't want to leave you boys, but before she left, she told me to tell you both how much she will always love you and how proud she was to be your mother.

She wanted both of you to know how much joy you gave her every day."

Ted looked at his father and realized that something had died inside him that day, and with their mother gone, their home would never know the love and joy it once had.

***

After his mother's death, the house felt cold and empty. They all missed her singing hymns while she cooked Sunday dinner and her smile when they would try to sneak a taste. They also missed her laughter when the boys would run to the kitchen, wanting to show her the frogs or snakes they just caught and wanted to keep as pets.

She would always tell them, "Boys, you need to realize that it's a living creature, and it deserves to be free to enjoy its life. Would you like to be kept in a jar or box every day? You can enjoy it for a little while, but then you need to set it free to go back to its life." Ted had always loved that about her; she would always put the feelings of others first.

Their father had spent long hours working the first six months after her death. He never wanted to talk about her or the baby, so the boys were careful not to bring them up in front of him. The only joy their father seemed to have was telling his old war stories. So, those evenings when there was nothing good to watch on the television, Ted and Jason would ask him to tell them the stories again.

Ted loved to listen to his father's stories. It did not matter how many times he had heard them; he enjoyed them each time as much as the first. "Dad, you're the best," he would always say.

***

Ted clearly remembered the day the news reached him of his father's death while he was in Vietnam. Upon returning from another messy patrol where they had lost several men, he had received a letter from his father's neighbor with the heartbreaking news. Ted knew the letter was not going to be the normal, "Hello" from home because the envelope did not have the usual silly little sayings written all over the backside of the envelope.

He held his breath and slowly opened it, not sure if he wanted to know its contents. *We regret to inform you of the death of your father. He passed away April 3rd from a massive heart attack. He went quickly, so we don't believe he suffered. We have also contacted your brother, and he will be here for the funeral on the 6th.*

Ted sat quietly for what seemed an eternity, just staring at the letter and not wanting to believe the words written on the page. He looked at the date written on the letter, "Damn, I missed it!"

For the rest of his tour in Vietnam, Ted began taking risks that he would never have before. If not for his friendship with Mack and Terry, he more than likely would have gotten himself killed.

The three of them had met when Ted first arrived in Vietnam, and they had become immediate friends. Mack Childers was the son of a small-town doctor from Wyoming. His father had wanted him to go to college and become a doctor as well; however, Mack had never liked school, so college was out of the question.

Mack's idea of the perfect life was to get on his horse and head up into the hills to hunt and camp out alone. He would always talk about the open skies of Wyoming and the endless herds of elk. Mack would tell Terry and Ted how they had to come for a visit after they all got back home because he would take them out for the best time of their lives.

Ted would laugh how Mack would get when it was close to hunting season. He would go on endlessly about how he wished he were home. "Damn, too bad I couldn't be there for at least a week. You've never tasted anything as good as a big, thick elk steak. Now that's some good eatin'!"

"Hell, don't you do enough killing? You being over here is probably the best thing for those poor ol' elk. At least it's giving them a chance to reproduce before you shoot them. Just think how many more of them will be there once you get home. Hell, there will be elk for as far as you can see!" Terry would always tease Mack.

"Yeah, I know, but you can't make a good steak out of what we kill over here," he laughed at the shocked look on Terry's face.

"Well, we could try it next time if you want to?" Terry grinned at the surprised look now on Mack's face.

"Hell, there isn't much meat on their bones, but who knows; they might be tasty?" Ted chimed in, and then laughed when he saw the shocked look now on both Terry and Mack's faces.

"I think Ted may be on to something!" Mack chuckled.

"Shit, you cowboys, will eat anything, won't you?" Terry groaned, fighting to get the mental picture out of his head.

"Sometimes," Mack grinned.

From that day forward, Mack was known as Cowboy.

***

Terry Smitten was from a wealthy family in New York City. From what Ted understood, Terry's father was a bigwig at a company on Wall Street, and his mother spent her time involved in charity work. Ted never understood why Terry had decided to join the Marine Corps, but Terry would merely say that he liked the Marine dress uniform, and he figured it would help him get the girls. Ted had always liked Terry; he had a great sense of humor and was always planning the next prank on some poor, unsuspecting victim. If there was something crazy going on, you could bet your last dollar that Terry was right in the middle of it.

Ted could distinctly remember the first time he had met Terry and Mack. He was walking to the mess tent for dinner when he noticed a small group of grunts huddled together, laughing and pointing at something.

As Ted walked over to see what was going on, he saw one of them staring down at his bare feet with a look of confusion on his face at his beautifully painted bright red toenails. Ted then looked to the right of the group where a tall, redheaded grunt was laughing so hard he could barely stand up while holding a bottle of red nail polish.

Ted wondered if this was something; he had done before by the satisfied look on his face.

"Man, you need to be careful where you fall asleep, and you also need to learn to sleep a little lighter. Hell, you never know who might sneak up on you," the redhead stated as he laughed and pointed to the confused soldier with the bright red toenails.

The young grunt looked at the one laughing with the bottle of polish, and calmly responded, "Man, it was raining like crazy earlier, and my feet got wet. I was only trying to dry them out, and I fell asleep in the warm sun." He looked down at the bright red on his toenails, feeling every bit the fool.

"Oh well, they do look a might pretty, don't they?" he said with a wink and a smile. This comment, of course, caused the entire group to break out into loud, rolling laughter.

Terry held out his hand to his victim and smiled, "They sure do, man. My name is Terry Smitten, from New York City. They call me Joker. I'm damn glad to meet you!"

"Glad to meet you, as well. I'm Mack Childers from Wyoming," he said, as he took Terry's hand and returned the firm handshake.

"Come on, Mack; let's go get something to eat, but first, you might want to put your boots back on before one of these grunts begins to think you're a little too pretty." Terry looked at the crowd of men gathered around, who was still laughing.

"Yeah, I hear that SOS is on the menu today. Man, that's my favorite!" Mack smacked his lips and patted his stomach. "It is almost as good as my momma makes back home."

"Crap, your momma must be a terrible cook," Terry laughed. "No wonder you joined up; you already have a cast-iron stomach."

With that comment, they all laughed and then walked toward the mess tent for their feast.

As Ted followed the group of men who would soon all go into battle, he wondered what lay ahead for them in this shithole corner of the world.

Chapter 3

"Man, how the hell can it rain so damn much? Shit, if I stay here much longer, I'm gonna grow webbed feet." Mack hated the wet weather in Vietnam. He would always say how he would rather have six feet of snow than all the rain.

They had been out on patrol for several days, and it had rained the entire time. It had been unusually quiet with no confrontation with the enemy, so they were all beginning to get a little aggravated, and short-tempered.

"Better watch out, Cowboy, you don't want to get your toenails all prettied up again," the grunt walking behind him teased.

"It wouldn't make any difference because I couldn't get the damn stuff off. Shit, it's still there!" Mack groancd, shaking his head at the memory of the bright red polish still on his toenails.

"Now, you just stay back because you're not my type." This comment brought the group to laughter.

"Come on, men, let's keep our minds on business," Sgt. Miller said in a stern voice. "We can all play later."

***

"Damn, I didn't know there could be so many trees in one place." Terry hated walking through the swamps.

"Shit, the vines grab you!" he groaned, pushing another one away.

"Yeah, you're only hoping it's a vine and not one of those damn snakes that hang around in here, and then drops down on you when you walk by!" Mack shuddered at the memory of the snake they had killed the day before.

Ted had to laugh how some of these men handled the wooded areas. Hell, he had grown up in the Great Thicket in Southeast Texas, so he was right at home walking through this shit. Ted had always enjoyed going deep into the woods hunting for deer and wild hogs, and his dad was always pleased when he came home with fresh meat.

He would always say, "Good job, Son, I was worried the freezer might be getting a little low on supplies."

It had been a while since his father had gone hunting. With arthritis in his legs from driving the logging truck all those years, it made it difficult for him to walk, so Ted had made sure to keep the freezer full of fresh meat.

Dad, you would get a kick out of these guys, Ted thought to himself as he pushed another vine out of the way.

***

"Oh shit!" A bullet ripped through Anderson's shoulder, knocking him to the ground, "I'm hit, I'm hit!"

"Get down, get down!" Sgt. Miller yelled. "Can anyone make his position?"

Another shot rang out.

"Thompson, he got Thompson!" Mack shouted.

Frank Thompson had only been in Vietnam for two weeks. He was a quiet young man, but friendly and got along with everyone.

"Oh man, the bastard shot him in the face, oh, my God!" Mack could not believe his eyes when suddenly a horrifying thought came to him. *Crap that could be me lying there!*

He then heard the buzz of another bullet, ending in a dull thud. "Shit, he almost got me!"

Terry watched the blood explode out of Mathew Dawson's chest. He reached over, placing his hand on the wound and tried to slow the gushing blood, but he knew from the look of death in Dawson's eyes that it was too late. "Can anyone make him? Where is he? If we don't get him soon, we're all dead."

Another shot rang out.

This one hit Sgt. Miller in the neck, knocking him back against a fallen tree. He reached for his throat and put his finger in the hole, trying to stop the gushing blood.

He opened his mouth to speak, but nothing came out except for gurgling and blood. He pointed to the radio and then to Ramirez, letting him know to call for help.

Ramirez grabbed the radio and began to dial-up when another shot rang out. This bullet hit Ramirez in the forehead, making a perfectly round entry hole. His body went rigid and then slumped backward over Sgt. Miller's legs. Ted knew that he would never forget the look of disbelief in Ramirez's eyes at the moment of his death.

Ted looked around him, and it was as if everything played out in some sort of slow-motion, silent movie. He knew there must be screaming, but the only thing he heard was the sound of his own beating heart. He looked around at the other men and saw the fear in their eyes. *I have to do something now!*

Another shot rang out.

There you are, you bastard! You should've quit while you were ahead.

When the last shot fired, Ted had noticed a small puff of smoke, come from behind a fallen tree, approximately twenty-five yards to the left of where he was crouching. *Now it's your turn to die,* he silently said to himself.

Back home, Ted used to love to sneak up on his brother, Jason, while they were out hunting. He had gotten quite good at making his way through the undergrowth without being seen or heard. Ted decided to leave everything behind except for his knife, so as not to make any unnecessary noise by trying to drag his rifle and gear.

Time to skin me a snake, he thought to himself.

***

The sniper never heard Ted come up from behind him. He was too busy enjoying the screams of all the dying men. The adrenaline surged through Ted's blood. Grabbing the sniper firmly, he placed the sharp blade of his knife against his throat.

"This is for my friends, enjoy hell," Ted whispered into the sniper's ear, as he slowly slit his throat.

Ted was surprised at how good he felt to make this kill. The smoothness of the blade, and how easily it cut through the skin, brought a smile to his lips. Ted only wished he could have seen the shooters face, as the blade sliced across his throat and the look of horror in his eyes once he realized he was dead.

The image of this in his mind made Ted chuckle, *Damn, that was better than killing one of those ole hogs back home.*

Ted snapped back to what was going on around him by the sound of a bullet buzzing just over his head.

"Hey, don't shoot! I'm a friendly; the sniper is terminated." Ted put his hands above his head and stood so they could clearly see him.

***

They had lost several good men that day, and others went home with life-changing injuries. Terry and Mack had joked how they would stay close to Ted for the rest of their time in Vietnam.

"Hell, it's good to have someone crazy enough to save our sorry asses in a pinch." Terry would say with Mack nodding in agreement. They both knew had it not been for Ted; more than likely that day, they all would have died. It was agreed that from that day forward, Ted was known as The Executioner.

Chapter 4

Ted awoke to a soft knocking at the door. "Housekeeping," the voice said from the other side of the door.

"One minute, please." Ted jumped out of bed and walked over to the door. "Can you come back in approximately fifteen minutes? I'll be out of here by then."

"No problem, Sir. Fifteen minutes, I come back," she replied, and then pushed her service cart to the next room.

Ted looked at his watch to see what time it was, "Shit, I'm a half-hour late!" He grabbed his clothes, threw them on, and ran out the door.

"I bet those assholes went ahead and ate without me," Ted laughed to himself as he ran down the three flights of stairs to the lobby.

He was walking past the lobby desk when he noticed two police officers standing there speaking with the clerk. One was an older man, and the other one looked as if he had recently graduated from the academy.

The clerk noticed Ted and motioned for him to stop, "Sir, please wait!"

What does he want with me? Ted thought to himself, but then an idea came to him. Maybe Mack and Terry had left a message for him.

Ted was sure they probably wanted to let him know they had eaten and gone on without him to explore the city.

That has to be it. I'm sure they want to let me know where to meet up with them, Ted thought to himself as he turned and walked to the desk.

"Do you have a message from those two knucklehead friends of mine?" Ted laughed.

The look on the desk clerk's face was serious. "Sir, these officers need to speak with you."

The clerk looked at the older officer and said, "You can talk in my office if you'd like." He turned and pointed to the door behind him.

Ted noticed that the clerk's voice sounded nervous, and his face seemed to grow paler by the moment.

"I think that might be a good idea," the older officer said.

Ted did not like how this was going. He had not done anything wrong, so why would the police want to talk to him. Suddenly a horrible thought came to him, *Terry and Mack!*

"No, if you have anything to say to me, say it right here." Ted stood rigid, waiting for the worst.

The two officers looked at each other, not sure of what to do. "We need you to come with us to the morgue," the older one finally said.

"Morgue, why do I need to go to the morgue?" Ted immediately got angry. He had seen enough death for one lifetime, and he did not want to see anymore.

"We need you to identify two bodies, Sir," the young officer said nervously. "We believe they were staying in this hotel with you."

Ted's mind spun wildly. "Don't you dare say it! You must be mistaken. Man, this is nothing to be joking about!" Ted said sharply, but he knew by the look on their faces, they were serious.

"Please, sir, we need identification from someone who knew them," the older officer murmured. The pleading look in his eyes let Ted know they were upset as well.

"All right, I'll go." Ted prayed it was a mistake, and that Terry and Mack were merely running around the city having the time of their lives, but he also knew that life does not always give us what we want.

***

It was the longest hallway Ted had ever walked down, and with each step, his mind kept arguing with him, *It is not them. You will get in there, and it won't be them.*

When they rounded the corner at the end of the hall, he saw the door with *Morgue* clearly printed on it. His breath caught in his chest, and a feeling of dread churned in the pit of his stomach at what could be behind the door.

The older officer reached for the door handle, opened the door, and waited for Ted. Ted hesitated a moment. Then he took a deep breath and stepped inside.

Once inside the room, Ted noticed how cold it was. Looking around the room, he saw six small labeled doors on the opposite wall. Ted then saw a door in the back corner of the room, which led to a small office where he saw a young man sat at a desk. Hearing the group enter the room, the young man stood and walked out to greet them.

"Good afternoon, I gather you're here to identify the bodics brought in earlier?" He turned and walked toward the small doors on the wall.

"Yes, this is Mr. Braxton. We believe he knew the victims," the older officer said while staring at the small doors on the wall.

The young man motioned to Ted to follow him. "Please stand right here. I need to warn you that what you are about to see will be a bit disturbing."

The young man reached for the handle of the first door, opened it, and pulled out the long tray with what appeared to be a body covered with a white sheet. He reached for the sheet and pulled it back to reveal the hidden nightmare.

The unimaginable vision lying there made Ted's blood run cold as ice, and a burning rage began to consume his soul.

***

The bar was dark, and cigarette smoke hung in the air. "Bartender, I'd like another one over here, and this time, make it a double," Ted groaned.

The vision of his friends still burned in Ted's mind. *How can that have happened?* He thought to himself, swallowing the last of his drink.

With everything, the three of us have been through the last year, to come home and die like that! "It's just not right!" he yelled, then slammed the glass down, sending the ice cubes dancing across the bar top, and onto the floor behind the bar.

"I think you've had enough, son." The bartender knew Ted was upset, but he did not want any trouble.

"I'm sorry; I'll hold it down." Ted did not want to leave. Hell, the last thing he needed now was to be out on the streets with the vision of Mack and Terry lying on that cold tray playing out in his mind. He knew he needed to stay right where he was, and calmly think of what to do next.

***

The official report stated extreme torture as the cause of death. The things done to them were beyond anything Ted could ever have imagined.

They each had their eyes removed and crushed on the pavement beside their bodies, and then their ears were burnt so severely that nothing was left but nubs. Both had *baby-killer* carved across their chests, and chunks of skin cut off their arms and legs. The worst was how each one had their genitals removed and forced into the other one's mouth.

Then they had their mouths sewn shut with fishing line. Then, to add additional insult, they had the word *fags* carved across their lower abdomens. The final act was the attackers had heated Mack and Terry's dog tags and burned them onto their foreheads.

This was how they identified the bodies; however, it was the hotel room key shoved up in Terry's anus that had led the authorities to Ted.

The report stated they had likely died slowly and in great pain. Ted kept asking if they had any idea who would have done this, but no one would give him a straight answer.

"I'm sorry, sir, we can't say anything. It's still an ongoing investigation, and since you're not a relative, we can't tell you more than you already know. Now that you've positively identified them, we'll contact their families. Once they're here, if they want to tell you any information, they're free to do so."

The detective in charge of the case could see the pain in Ted's eyes. "I know you all had recently come back from the war, and I can't begin to tell you how sorry I am this happened. Many things have changed since you left. There's a lot of unrest about our involvement in the war, and there are angry people out there willing to make their political statement by killing a soldier. I guarantee you that we will do everything we can to catch and punish the animals that did this to your friends; you have my word."

Ted knew the officer wanted to catch the people who had killed Mack and Terry, but he also knew that the law, at times, does not give us the justice we desire.

***

Everything felt strange when Ted returned home to Southeast Texas. The house was empty, and he found himself staying to himself most of the time. Over the last four months since his return, Ted had worked for the mill, driving his father's truck. He worked long hours trying to erase the memories of Vietnam, but each night the vision of Terry and Mack lying on a cold metal tray haunted his dreams.

He was thankful the war protesters were not in his little corner of the country. He would watch them on the television in the evenings, and it made him sick.

Damn, dirty fools. They have no idea what's going on in Vietnam. Don't they understand they're making it worse for us over there? Support the soldiers, my ass!

Ted was thankful that Mack and Terry's families had kept him updated on the progress of the investigation. With the arrest two months earlier of four members of a militant anti-war group, it seemed as though things were finally coming to an end.

The manifesto of the group stated the United States was guilty of war crimes, and the military was guilty of the murder of thousands of innocent Vietnamese citizens.

The press, of course, had glossed over the entire ordeal by not once mentioning the torture of Terry or Mack. Ted was stunned how the press had held up the members of the group as folk heroes, fighting against a corrupt government to free the world from tyranny.

Mack's father had kept Ted up to date on the case as much as possible. He would send copies of the local newspapers and notes he had written detailing the daily court proceedings.

Son, I'm worried they're going to get away with it; Mr. Childers had stated in his last letter.

They have a slick lawyer, and it looks as though the police may have botched several important parts of the investigation. Today, they threw out some of the best evidence that connected them to the murders. They said it was something about not filing the proper paperwork, but I have my suspicions. My wife had to go home last week because she couldn't handle it anymore. As for Mr. and Mrs. Smitten, they're still here even though they do not sit in the courtroom every day. We were all surprised today when Mr. Smitten had to be forcibly removed from the courtroom because he could no longer stand the smug looks on the faces of those animals. They were always looking over at us and sneering. I thought Mr. Smitten was going to jail today for sure. He jumped up and began yelling how they needed to die the same way his son did. He then looked at the judge and said it was nothing more than a kangaroo court, and if those murderers walked free, he would hunt them down until his dying days.

Ted wished he had been there to see that because he felt the same way. *With all the evidence stacked against them, how could it be possible that any court would set those murdering assholes free?*

However, deep in his heart, he knew there was a good chance they might just get away with   it.

Chapter 5

Ted was exceptionally tired. He had started out early in the morning at work and ended up pulling several extra loads. He was trying to make money for his trip to San Francisco for the last days of the trial, so he was glad for the extra work.

Mr. Childers had written to him how it looked as if the trial was ending, and it was not going well at all. He had written how, on the previous Wednesday, Mr. Smitten went to the hospital with chest pains, and he was still there recovering. He went on to say how Mrs. Smitten was beside herself with worry and refused to leave his side. Mr. Childers also stated that he did not have the heart to notify her of the new developments in the trial. She had said that she did not want Mr. Smitten to get any more upset then he was already.

It had been an exceptionally long day when Ted pulled the truck around to the back of the house, gathered his things, and headed to the kitchen door.

Shit, I left the damn kitchen light on this morning, he thought to himself as he walked up the sidewalk.

As he reached for the doorknob, the door swung open. "Crap, you scared the shit out of me!" Ted groaned while he tried to catch his breath.

Michael Rathburn had been a long-time friend and neighbor of Ted's family. He was the one who had written to him about his father's death and had taken care of all the funeral arrangements. Ted was grateful for everything he and his wife, Carolyn, had done for him during that difficult time.

After his father's death, Jason had gone to Basic Training, and they had kept an eye on the place. When Jason shipped out to Vietnam just before Ted came home, they had made sure everything was cared for until Ted's return.

Mr. Rathburn had kept the truck and trailer maintained while also keeping the tags and insurance current. He knew how important the truck was to Ted's dad, so he wanted to be sure it was in top condition when Ted returned home from the war.

He would tell Ted in letters, *"Don't worry about the money, son. Once you return home and get to work, you can pay me back. I know it would make your dad proud for you to take over for him, so I go over there once a week to make sure it stays clean and in working order. You know how much your dad meant to us, so I don't ever want you to feel it's an imposition. Just come home safe because we miss seeing that ole truck going up and down the highway."*

***

This can't be happening again. Not Jason, too, Ted thought to himself. He read the telegram one more time, staring at the page, not wanting to believe the words.

We regret to inform you, was in the opening statement. "He's gone," Ted said to himself, realizing how everyone he had ever loved in this screwed up world was gone.

He had known when he saw the look on Mr. Rathburn's face it was not going to be good news. Mrs. Rathburn was washing the dishes he had left in the sink that morning, trying to hide her tears when he walked into the kitchen. She could not bring herself to look in his direction while he read the telegram.

"Son, you need to sit down. You know we're here for you, no matter what you need, right?" the sadness was evident in Mr. Rathburn's voice.

"I know; I need some time alone to think things through." Ted did not want to be around anyone. With his world destroyed, Ted had no clue how to control the rage growing inside of him.

***

The next few days were some of the loneliest Ted had ever known. Nothing seemed to erase the empty feeling in his soul, and driving that ole truck only made him think of happier days with his dad and brother. Then at night, he would see the bodies of Mack and Terry lying on that cold metal tray in his dreams.

Life was easier in the jungles of Vietnam because you didn't have time to dwell on old memories.

***

The letter arrived five days before Ted was to leave for San Francisco, and the words *NOT GUILTY* burned into his mind.

"How could that happen?" Ted groaned.

Mr. Childers had stated he knew it was going to happen the moment the judge told the jury to disregard all the evidence thrown out during the trial, and only consider the case before them.

"Hell, there wasn't any case left; their damn lawyer had made sure of that!" Ted said aloud, but the real deciding factor was the newspaper article about the interview with the judge touting how justice was served.

The judge then went on to say, *"It has always been my goal to ensure anyone who sits accused in my court receives a fair and impartial trial. Just because you may not agree with their political views, as citizens of the United States of America, they have a constitutional right to voice it. I'm proud of the fact the people are speaking out because this is what makes our country unique."*

Ted stared at the article. *Rights, what rights did they give to Mack and Terry?* He thought to himself, as anger churned in the pit of his stomach.

In the letter, Mr. Childers stated that when Mr. Smitten learned of the verdict, he had another heart attack, and they were not sure if he would survive.

"This has destroyed too many lives. Mr. Smitten had tried to leave the hospital upon hearing the verdict, and it had taken two large orderlies to hold him down. Poor Mrs.

Smitten is beside herself with grief. She keeps saying how she cannot go on without him, and how it would be too much to lose them both. I spoke with Mr. Smitten's nurse, and she said he kept yelling, I'll show you justice! I'll kill the bastards the same way they murdered my boy! She said she understood his grief as her little sister was raped a couple of years earlier, and nothing was ever done about it. The investigators in the case had decided her sister brought it on herself. The nurse asked me how could an eleven-year-old girl, while walking home from school, cause a pervert to grab her and throw her in a van. Then how was it her fault that he repeatedly raped her until she was so torn up inside that she'd never have children? I wish someone would do something about the animals that keep getting away with committing these horrible crimes. It makes me sick how the lawyers and judges are more worried about protecting the guilty than they are of protecting the innocent victims. Justice, there is no justice anymore!"

Those words burned into Ted's mind all night. *He's right; there is no justice for the innocent anymore.*

"I know what I have to do," he said to himself as he reached for his duffel bag and began to pack.

Chapter 6

The fog had finally lifted, allowing the airplane to land at the San Francisco International Airport. Several times, Ted had gone over in his mind what he planned to do, but he knew it would not be easy.

Before leaving home, he had left instructions that the house, truck, trailer, everything was to be signed over to Mr. and Mrs. Rathburn. As far as Ted was concerned, they were the closest thing he had left to a family. He also knew this way he would be able to repay them for everything they had done for his family throughout the years. Ted knew he would never come back, and, to be honest, he did not want to return.

Ted had told the Rathburn's not to look for him, and the reason he was leaving was that he did not wish to stay in a house filled with all the memories of his parents and brother. He then told them to sell everything and do whatever they thought best with the money. The only things he took with him were his father's old hooded work coat and a few pictures from happier times.

***

As he walked through the airport, he noticed a small group of anti-war protesters heckling some returning soldiers. The looks on the faces of the soldiers were of disbelief and shock, as the protesters chanted, *Baby killers! Baby killers!*

Ted then saw one of the protestors throw something at one of the soldiers, hitting him in the face. That was when things exploded out of control. The protesters defiantly stood their ground as the soldiers turned to face them. After several tense-filled moments, the protesters began throwing objects at the soldiers and screaming, *Murderers! Traitors!*

This caused the group of soldiers to move in on the protesters in a full-on attack. Ted watched as the airport security officers charged forward, trying to break up the commotion, but things were completely out of control.

People were yelling and throwing whatever they could get their hands on in a wild fury. Ted watched as one of the soldiers hit a protester so hard in the face that blood splattered all over innocent bystanders, causing howls of protest. Before Ted could react, the security officers had drawn their batons and began hitting anyone within reach; thus causing the protesters to cower like beaten dogs, crying and pleading for mercy.

Ted could not believe how the airport security would allow protesters to hang around, causing problems for the returning soldiers, but he realized that things had most assuredly changed since he left for Vietnam. During the skirmish, he heard one of the protesters screaming about how his freedom of speech was being violated.

That wasn't freedom of speech; it was inciting a riot. What has happened to this country? Ted wondered to himself.

Don't those idiots realize they wouldn't have their precious freedom of speech if it weren't for the sacrifice of our soldiers?

Ted was glad his father was not alive to see this. *"Dad, I promise that I'll do everything I can to bring justice back to this country. I won't let what you fought for in the Great War ever to be forgotten. You fought against tyranny and the injustice of a foreign aggressor. Now it's time to protect this country from those on our own soil."*

He turned and walked away with a renewed strength and conviction.

***

It had been one of the roughest afternoons Ted had ever known. He had gone directly to the hotel where Mr. Childers was packing for his flight back to Wyoming the next morning.

"You know, it's been a comfort staying in the last room my Mackie stayed in. Sometimes late at night, I can feel him here with me. You know something, I'll never understand any of this, Ted. How can they let those..., how can they simply walk away unpunished?"

He fought back the tears, but the pain was too much for him. "Those boys never had a chance. To come back from the war only to be murdered by your own countrymen is so unfair. How could they do those horrible things to my Mackie?" The agony filled emotions washed over him to the point where he could no longer speak.

Ted did not know what to say to ease Mr. Childer's pain. Hell, he had no idea how to ease his own pain. Rage ate away at his soul, like cancer, of which there seemed to be no cure.

"Sir, I don't understand it myself, but I promise you and Mrs. Childers will finally know justice for Mack. You have my word."

Mr. Childers looked deep into Ted's eyes, seeing the conviction firmly there, and nodded his understanding. "Thank you," were the only words spoken.

**

Darkness enveloped the hospital room, with the only light from a small lamp on the bedside table. Mrs. Smitten was sleeping in the chair across from the bed with her feet propped up on a folding chair. She was a delicate woman with soft, curly red hair and her fair skin. He could see how Terry had favored her.

Ted's heart ached for the pain clearly etched across her sleeping face. To lose everyone you love is more than anyone should ever have to endure.

The only sound in the room was the heart monitor, as it counted each heartbeat. *Beep, beep, beep*.

Ted stepped into the room and quietly closed the door behind him. The last thing he wanted was for the night nurse to realize that he had snuck past her station, as visiting hours had ended long ago. He had waited for her to go into one of the other rooms then quickly made his way down the hall to Mr. Smitten's room.

Ted stood silently, looking down at Mr. Smitten, praying he would regain his health and be able to go on with his life. He looked so frail, and Ted wondered how much longer he would be able to hang on to this life.

After a few moments, he slowly opened his eyes and looked up at Ted.

"Ted, is that you?" his voice was raspy as he strained to talk.

"Yes, Sir, it is." Ted leaned closer to hear him better.

"They let them go. Why would they let them go?" The frustration and anger clearly shown in his eyes.

"I don't know, Sir." Ted wanted to yell at the top of his voice the injustice of it all, but he merely held Mr. Smitten's gaze.

"They need to pay! They can't destroy lives like that, and not pay! I can't do anything while I'm like this, please...," his voice trailed off, but Ted knew what he wanted to say.

"Sir, I promise that they will pay. You will know justice for Terry's death; rest assured of that, Sir." Ted looked deeply into Mr. Smitten's eyes, feeling his anguish.

A smile formed at the corners of his mouth. "Thank you. I can rest now," holding Ted's gaze, a small tear formed in the corner of his eye.

"Terry was lucky to have you as a friend." He then closed his eyes, and for the first time in months, enjoyed a peaceful slumber.

Chapter 7

"Sir, I have an envelope for you," the night clerk announced when Ted came back to the hotel.

Who would leave me an envelope? Ted thought to himself.

He walked to the desk and took it from the clerk. "Thank you."

He looked at the thick, yellow envelope and noticed there was nothing more than his name written across the front. Curious about its contents, he headed for the stairs leading up to his room, wondering what he would find.

***

"Well, I'll be damned. It's all here."

Ted was surprised at what he found when he returned to his room and emptied the contents of the envelope on the table. Inside were newspaper articles and handwritten notes from all the court proceedings. He was pleased with the detail of the notes, as they contained all the names, places, and descriptions needed to fulfill his promise. He was also glad to see the newspaper included pictures of the defendants taken the day of the acquittal.

In one of the newspapers, the reporter began the article with the headline, "*Justice Served!*" The reporter then went on to explain how the defendants were cleared of all charges, and the system had proven to be just.

At seeing the smiles on their faces, in the picture, Ted's blood began to boil. "You won't be smiling for long."

Ted ended up working all night, carefully studying all the notes and pictures until he knew each name and detail by memory.

"Now I'm ready," he said, as he noticed the morning sun peeking through the bedroom curtains.

He rubbed his eyes and placed everything back into the envelope. "Mr. Childers, you have given me everything I need to fulfill my promise. They will finally pay for what they did to Mack and Terry."

Ted looked around the room one last time, making sure he had not forgotten anything. He then gathered his things and walked to the door.

Time to get to work, he said silently to himself. Then after closing the door behind him, he walked to the stairs.

***

"Good Morning, Mr. Braxton, how are you doing today? Are you planning to visit any of the sites in the city today?" The clerk asked, trying his best to muster a smile.

"No, I'll be checking out. I'm going home." Ted reached into his wallet to pay for his bill.

"Oh, Sir, there's no need for that. Mr. Childers has already paid for your room for as long as you want to stay. He had made the arrangements this morning before he checked out to fly home," the desk clerk smiled.

"If you're sure," he smiled, then reached for the registration book.

"I'm positive. I need to get out of this damn city," Ted groaned, with a look of anger clearly showing on his face.

"Here's the key to the room." He handed the key to the desk clerk, turned, and walked toward the front door without saying another word.

"Sir, I'm sorry about your friends; they didn't deserve what happened to them," the clerk said with sadness evident in his voice.

"You're right; they didn't." Without another word, Ted opened the door and stepped out into the new day.

Chapter 8

What a disgusting place to live, Ted thought to himself.

He could tell this part of the city had once been a beautiful place but was now overrun with nothing but hippies and bums.

"Shit, they live like a bunch of cockroaches."

Ted was unaccustomed to people sleeping wherever they wanted or staying drugged up to the point that they had no clue where they were, let alone who they were.

He also did not understand how anyone could be so selfish. They would go around chanting thinks like, *Make love, not war, and Hell no, we won't go* without understanding how they even got the freedom to act such fools.

What the hell, kind of crap is that? He thought to himself.

Ted had grown up to believe in pride for one's self and country.

Dad would have kicked our butts if we acted like this; he chuckled.

The sight of them made Ted's skin crawl, but he knew he would have to infiltrate their culture, to accomplish his mission.

***

To Ted's surprise, it turned out to be easier to do than he had expected. In no time, he was fortunate enough to meet a small group of anti-war protesters, thrilled to find a soldier wanting to protest the war.

Gullible assholes, he thought to himself as they patted him on the back for having the courage to turn his back on the murdering government and military.

He told them with stories of how the government had ordered them to kill innocent women and children, and then how they would all laugh while the crying mothers begged for the lives of their babies. He went on with the most unbelievable tales of murder and carnage, but the damn fools sat transfixed, clinging to his every word.

Sometimes he would look at the group and wonder when they would call his bluff, but no one ever did. They wanted his lies to be the truth, and they believed every one of them no matter how ridiculous they were.

Their damn brains are so fried from all the drugs that they have no clue what's going on; he laughed to himself.

While in Vietnam, Ted had seen the results of using drugs by several of the other soldiers. *The shit makes you crazy and out of control.*

He had tried some pot once while out on patrol, but he did not enjoy it. "The stuff tasted like shit. Hell, give me a stiff shot of whiskey, and a good cigar anytime over that crap!" he would always say.

Ted knew that he had to be careful whenever he was around this group because they were always trying to slip him one drug or another.

One night he brought some hand-rolled cigarettes to a gathering to smoke instead of marijuana. When a girl sitting next to him grabbed one out of his hand and took a long drag on it, Ted could not help but laugh.

The look of surprise on her face was priceless. She had coughed and gagged so much that Ted thought she would pass out cold. Then, once she composed herself, she proceeded to inform the others of the intense high it had given her while offering it to the rest of the group. After several minutes of coughing and choking, they all laid back to enjoy their high from this new weed.

Ted had spent several days with this group and still had no leads on the ones who had killed Mack and Terry. He had finally decided it was time to move on when he got the break he had been waiting to come.

One night, a couple of new guys had shown up at the gathering looking for people to attend a big protest at the military recruiting office downtown. They said it was time to hit The Man hard, and that they wanted to make sure no more Americans turned into Murderers of the Innocent.

"He was there! He knows what's going on," the young girl sitting to the right of Ted cried out as she pointed towards him.

"He hates The Man, as much as we do; maybe even more," she exclaimed with more energy than Ted had seen her show the entire evening.

"She's right, he does," another girl sitting next to her added.

Suddenly, Ted felt all eyes were on him. He had been working toward this moment, so he knew he would have to remain calm and detached. He slowly looked up at the two men, as though their presence was of no consequence to him.

"They're right; I hate The Man. They forced me to kill more people than I care to remember. I still feel their blood all over me."

Both men looked at Ted, trying to decide if he was for real or not.

After a few tense moments, the tall one spoke, "What were you over there?"

"1st Marine Recon," Ted spoke slowly, choosing his words carefully.

"Thought I was serving my country, but I don't see the point of what we're doing over there. I came home wanting to cleanse myself of the horrible acts I committed, but my family didn't understand why I had changed. They said they didn't want a traitor in the family, so I left. I watched too many of my friends die over there for something I can no longer support."

Ted prayed that they believed him because the words were poison on his tongue. However, he knew to get in with the ones who had killed Mack and Terry; he needed to convince them that he was now one of them.

Several long and tense moments of silence passed as they tried to read each other's thoughts.

Finally, the other one spoke, breaking the stalemate. "Do you want to help end the war? If you do, we have a plan to bring the government to its knees."

Ted held firm, refusing to break eye contact, "Yes, I would. I need to cleanse my soul of all the blood. I'm ready to fight for what is right this time."

"Wonderful, I think you're just what we've been waiting for to make this attack on the Man. What's your name? I'm Ron," he stepped forward and offered his hand.

Ted held out his hand and took Ron's in a firm handshake, "They call me The Executioner."

A smile appeared on Ron's lips. *Yes, he's precisely the type of recruit we need.* "Welcome to the resistance, Executioner."

Chapter 9

The twenty-minute ride seemed to last an eternity. Ted had sat quietly in the back seat, doing his best, not to make eye contact with the others. As Ron drove the old, beat-up Impala, he kept a close eye on Ted through the rear-view mirror while the others in the car talked amongst themselves.

Ron wondered if Ted was what he had proclaimed to be, but he had to admit that he was thrilled at the prospect that he was.

The girl in the front next to Ron had fallen asleep five minutes after they got in the car and was mumbling something in her sleep. It did not surprise Ted that she had fallen asleep so quickly since she had smoked quite a bit of marijuana and taken a couple of Quaaludes before they left. Ted finally closed his eyes, hoping this would get Ron to quit staring at him.

Several minutes passed when they finally stopped in front of an old, rundown building.

"Thank goodness we're here," the one sitting next to Ted groaned as he slid out of the door. "I hate being closed up like that."

Ted was glad to get out of the car as well. The smell of marijuana mixed with the body odor on their clothes, was beginning to make him nauseous.

"Come on, it wasn't that bad. Hell, you need to try living in the jungles of Vietnam for a while. Now that will make you appreciate having a car to get around in," Ted forced a smile, and then elbowed the one complaining.

"He's right, Tony; knock off your damn whining." Ron did not know why he put up with Tony, every time they made plans, he would always complain.

"Come on, let's get inside; the others are waiting. Charlene, get your lazy ass out of the car!" Ron slammed his fist on the window, trying to wake her up, but she did not move.

"Forget her. The stupid bitch can sleep in the car for all I care," he laughed as he walked toward the door with the others following behind him.

***

How can things get any worse? Ted thought to himself.

The smell of rotting food and stale smoke filled his nostrils once he stepped inside the warehouse, causing his stomach to churn. Ignoring the stench, the best he could, he looked around the large room, taking a mental note of everything.

First, he noticed the old mattresses lying around the room, covered with torn and dirty blankets, and then the several small wooden spindles placed around the room as tables. He noticed the tables covered with all sorts of drug paraphernalia that any drug addict would want or need. He saw needles, pipes, bags of marijuana with zigzag paper packets, and small foil pouches of what he assumed were Black Tar Heroin.

He looked around again and counted seven people in the room. Five of them were lying on the scattered mattresses, probably tripping on whatever drug they had taken.

At one of the spindle tables were two men who were passing a smoke-filled pipe between them, but what captured Ted's attention was the table across the room covered with weapons of all types.

This has to be the ones I've been looking for; Ted smiled.

"Rat, come here. I've found just what we've been looking for." Ron called out to one of the men sitting at the spindle table in the corner.

"Put that shit down, it's time to get serious. I believe that I've have found what we need to put our plan in motion."

Ted watched a small man with a sharp, pointed nose and a long, stringy goatee stand and walk over to join them. His tattered clothes and filthy skin looked as though he had not taken a bath in quite some time.

It makes sense why they call him Rat; Ted thought to himself.

Rat had never trusted strangers, and for some reason, he took an instant dislike to Ted. Looking him up and down, Rat walked toward Ted until he stood only inches away from him. Ted towered over Rat, forcing Ted to look down to meet his gaze.

They both stood still for several tense-filled moments with neither blinking until Ron finally broke the standoff.

"Knock that crap off, Rat! He's like you; a soldier who discovered he was committing murder for The Man, and now wants to set things right."

Rat paused a moment then moved in closer, testing the moment. Knowing this was the only chance he had to prove himself, Ted leaned down with his face nearly touching Rats; their eyes burning into each other. Neither of them blinked nor took a breath until SLAM!

They all turned to see the man left at the spindle table lying face down on the floor, and everything that was on the table now scattered across the floor. Of course, that ended the standoff, as roars of laughter erupted from the others, who only moments before were watching Ted and Rat.

"Shit, Todd, you're going to kill yourself someday," Tony laughed, trying to catch his breath.

"Tony, go help your dumbass friend get up. Shit, I sure hope he didn't break anything. The idiot never knows when he's had enough. The damn fool stays stoned all the fucking time!" Ron groaned and then gestured to Tony to go and help Todd.

Ron returned his attention to Ted and Rat. "Are you two done yet? Come on, let's get down to business."

Ron pushed past the two of them and walked to the door in the back of the room.

Rat took one final look at Ted and then turned to follow Ron.

There's something off about this guy, Rat thought to himself.

Ted took another glance at Todd, who was still lying on the floor. "Damn fool probably doesn't have a brain cell left in his head," Ted snickered and then turned to follow Ron.

Ted never did understand why people enjoyed being out of control like that. He had done it only once in his life. It was the night he drove his pickup truck into a tree, and almost killed himself and Billy Pontrey.

***

Ted and Billy had been out one evening during their junior year in high school. They were drinking and spotlighting deer when Ted misjudged a curve and ran into Mr. Sander's old oak tree. *I sure did catch a load of crap over that stunt.* Not only had he nearly killed himself and Billy, but he had put one hell of a gouge in the old oak tree.

Mr. Sanders chewed on both of us about how that tree was there since his great-grandfather came to Texas from Kentucky, and how it was around when Texas became a state. I'll never forget the look on his face when he said that old tree had watched over his family for well over one hundred years.

He damn sure didn't want a couple of foolish, snot-nosed kids killing his family's tree. I was relieved when the old man told us that he wouldn't press charges for the damage as long as we worked on his ranch every Saturday for the remainder of the school year.

Ted smiled at the memory of those days. He would never admit it at the time, but he had enjoyed working for Mr. Sanders. The two of them would show up early on Saturday morning and work until sundown, but Ted did not mind it at all. He would never forget the Saturday when they spent the afternoon running the new fence in the back pasture. It was hard work, but Ted felt a sense of pride when he stood back and looked at what they had accomplished.

Billy, on the other hand, had hated everything about ranching. He had gone on endlessly of the blisters on his hands, and how he knew he would have them the rest of his life.

Ted thought back to the time when they were digging up some old stumps, and Billy got into a fire ant mound.

The look on his face, as those little bastards began to bite him, was priceless, Ted chuckled silently.

Billy had taken off running as if his hair was on fire, screaming and doing a strange dance while he fought to get the burning attackers off his legs and out of his shoes.

Ted had warned him to wear jeans and boots, but Billy would not have anything to do with it.

"It's too hot, they'll only make it worse," Billy had protested, but from that Saturday forward, Billy Pontrey showed up for work in jeans and boots.

***

"Come over here and have a seat," Ron said, pulling Ted back to the present.

Ted looked around and noticed pictures from newspapers and a chalkboard with strange diagrams drawn on it lining the walls of the small room.

This must be their planning room, he thought to himself as he walked into the room and sat in the offered chair.

Ron sat at the head of the table, and Rat took a seat across from Ted. A few moments later, Tony walked into the room, helping a stunned Todd. They both sat at the end of the table closest to the door.

Ron looked at the group seated at the table and began. "Well, let's get the introductions out of the way first. You've already met Tony and Rat. Then you saw Todd earlier," Ron said to Ted.

"We all know everyone at the table except for him!" Rat interrupted while glaring at Ted. He did not want to waste any more time on pleasantries, and for some reason, Ted made him feel uneasy.

"Let's have your name," he glared at Ted, daring him again.

"Knock that crap off, Rat!" Ron slammed his fist down on the table.

Ted came to full alert. He knew he must earn the trust of all the members before he would be able to fulfill his plan.

"No problem, man. I understand his mistrust. The Man messed with his head the same way he did with mine. I don't have a name. I gave it up when my so-called family disowned me for turning against the war, and this screwed up country."

Ted hated the taste of the words as they left his mouth, but he pressed on. "My ole man told me not ever to come back home, and that

I was no longer his son. For this reason, I left, and I've been on my own ever since. My dead brothers in Nam gave me a new name; they called me, The Executioner."

"Shit, Executioner? What kind of name is that?" Todd's eyes were wider now than they had been in months.

"It's what I do. I kill, I'm good at it, and I enjoy it," Ted said flatly.

Todd began to say something else when Ron interrupted him. "That's what we need now to drive our message home. We have to do something grand, something that will draw attention to the cause. We only put a small dent in the establishment by killing those two soldiers a few months back."

Rat laughed at this statement. "Yeah, I sure wish I could have been there to help because they sure sent a message with those two. It was too easy; the damn fools never saw it coming. Of course, with the stupid pigs messing up the case from the very beginning, it was a complete victory for the cause." The rest of the group all voiced their agreement and pleasure with the outcome.

Ted's blood began to boil at the confirmation of his suspicions. *I've found the group responsible for killing Mack and Terry!*

He looked at Rat and saw pleasure dancing in his eyes. *I'll have the most fun watching you die;* Ted thought to himself.

Learning that a fellow soldier took part in their murders caught Ted completely by surprise, and he decided to make Rat pay for his involvement in a way that only he would understand.

Rat looked at Ted, reading the troubled look in his eyes. "What's the matter? Does it bother you that two baby killers died? They deserved what they got. In fact, Dean said they begged for mercy until he choked them with each other's dicks! The pussies died sucking cock!"

Rat loved to tell this story. He would always laugh at the mental picture it created for him.

Ted fought the desire to leap across the table and kill the slimy little bastard. "No, it doesn't bother me. I've killed several of those types myself before I came back to the world. Taking out a flag-waver was easy. Hell, all you had to do was get yourself in a gun battle, and well, you know how shit happens. I decided the best way to help the war end faster was by increasing the body count. You understand me, don't you?" Ted said, looking directly into Rat's eyes.

"I know you enjoyed killing over there, didn't you? You would climb right down in those tunnels and flush the little bastards out, wouldn't you?"

This statement brought Rat up straight in his chair, with his eyes burning into Ted's. However, this response only drove Ted onward.

"We all loved little guys like you. Yep, you tunnel rats sure did come in handy. I never did understand how you all kept from going crazy, though, sliding down into those dark, snake-infested holes, not knowing if you would ever see the sun again. Man, you guys had balls!"

Ted paused for effect, and then he continued. "It must have fucked you up to know you were disposable like that. How many of you died down there, only to have your brothers leave you behind buried in the dark, cold ground?"

Ted knew those men were necessary and never treated lightly. However, the look on Rat's face clearly showed that he was bothered by this part of his past, so he pressed on. "I guess every army needs its disposable men."

Rat could no longer control his anger. "I'll kill you!" he yelled.

He jumped to his feet and climbed across the table toward Ted, the rage burning in his eyes.

"Sit down, Rat!" Ron shouted as he reached to stop him. "You two can have your little pissing match on your own time. Now sit down and shut up because we have plans to work on."

***

"What the hell is going on in here?" a voice laughed from the doorway. "Shit, you'd think the war had moved in here."

Ted turned to see four men walk into the room, and once they sat at the table, Ted was able to see their faces. *These are the assholes who killed Mack and Terry!*

Ted could not believe the men who murdered Mack, and Terry was sitting mere inches away from him, and it took every ounce of his strength, not to slaughter the four of them on the spot. *Control yourself, Ted; it's not the right time yet.*

The one sitting next to Rat looked at Ted. *He's a strange-looking man*, Ted thought to himself.

His hair was long and frizzy, and he had an Amish-style beard. Ted noticed how he was trying to hide an acne problem with the beard, but it only drew more attention to the redness.

"Who's this? I've never seen him around here before," Dean asked while looking at Ted.

He then looked at Ron, "Is this one of your new recruits?"

"As a matter of fact, he is, and he's precisely the type we've been looking for too. He was 1st Marine Recon and is just what we need for our next project," Ron smiled at Dean.

Dean nodded in agreement. "He sure is; he's just what we've been waiting for."

Chapter 10

The rest of the meeting was excruciating for Ted. To sit that close to Mack and Terry's murderers was almost more than he could bear. At least no one expected him to add anything to the conversation, of which he was grateful.

Joel and Ray had joined the fray with their desire to kill every soldier they could.

"They make me sick with the things they do over there. They aren't even human," Joel said, while he looked at Ted, waiting for a response.

Ted sat and listened to the conversation without saying a word. Of course, this made Ray nervous.

"Did you kill any women and children over there?" Ray had bought into all the propaganda spewed by the anti-war protesters, as well as the media. He had heard the stories of soldiers killing children the same way you would an unwanted animal.

It did not matter to Ray that the children had grenades hidden in their diapers and were left as bait for some unsuspecting American soldier to get himself blown up along with the child. The Vietcong knew the Americans were suckers for a helpless child, and they used it to their advantage every chance they could.

Ted thought back to the time he watched a young grunt from Nebraska try to save a baby boy by doing everything he could to remove a grenade from the child's diaper before it exploded.

The damn fool got himself blown up right along with the kid, the words screamed in Ted's mind. Unfortunately, this group was convinced the Americans were at fault for the children's deaths.

"I may have once or twice, but what does that have to do with today? If you feel the need to press for details of my time over there, then this isn't the place for me. I don't want to talk about it, and there are things I'd rather put out of my mind forever." Ted began to stand, but Ron motioned for him to sit.

"Shut the hell up, Ray, and leave him alone. I'm sorry about that; Ray can be a real asshole at times. I understand why you don't want to remember your time over there, and I can't blame you. The things they made you do must really eat at you," Ron smiled, hoping this would put Ted at ease.

"Please, you are among brothers here, and you can redeem your soul by striking back at the ones who stole it. Look at Rat there. He came to us broken and with no direction. We took him in and showed him the way, and we can do the same for you," Ron looked deep into Ted's eyes, trying to reassure him.

Ted had waited for this response, as this proved his acceptance as one of the group. *It's all starting to come together,* he thought to himself.

***

The rest of the evening, they spent planning their next mission. Ted was shocked to learn that they planned to hit a Recruiting Office and to murder the Recruiting Officer. The plan was to strap him to a chair and burn him alive in front of the Recruiting Office. However, first, they would notify the media to make sure the television cameras were there to broadcast it on the evening news.

Ted was sickened to learn his role in this mission. They knew none of them could get into the office without causing suspicion, but now that he had joined the group, the plan could move forward. He was the *in* they had been waiting to come.

"He'll never suspect you because you still have that look about you," Ron laughed at how it was coming together.

"He'll take one look at you and want to sign you right up!" This statement caused the rest of the group to roll with laughter.

"Yeah, and when he least expects it, you will knock him out," Steve chimed, his eyes burning with excitement.

"Sure, wish it was me going in there. I'd love to hear him begging for his pathetic life. Hell, I enjoyed ripping the eyes out of those other ones and then watching their ears burn and fall off, as they begged for mercy," Steve laughed.

"It was a work of art," Ray added to the conversation.

"What about Joel's handy work? He carved them up like a patchwork quilt," Ray laughed, slapping his hand on the table.

"Ah, thanks, man, but you and Dean did the real masterpiece. The memory of their cut off dicks crammed into each other's mouths is one I'll treasure forever. That will be a hard one to top," Ray laughed at the memory of that morning.

"Yeah, the horny little peckerheads had no idea they were being set up. Charlene and Willow led them right to us," Steve laughed.

"They sure were distracted, weren't they?" Joel chimed in.

"They sure were. You'd think they would've learned to pay better attention to their surroundings while they were over there in Vietnam. I guess when you're getting your dick sucked, you don't care, huh?" Dean laughed, remembering how quickly Mack and Terry fell into their trap.

Steve leaned over and elbowed Dean. "I've had Willow suck my cock, and she can make you forget everything with that tongue of hers," he snickered, as he winked at Dean.

Ted sat and carefully listened to every detail, said, fighting to contain the rage burning deep inside of him. They sat there and talked about Terry and Mack as if they were nothing and laughed how they had inflicted so much pain on them. Ted had often wondered how Mack and Terry managed to get caught off guard.

So, two of the girls in the group had lured them into a trap. The damn fools never saw it coming.   Hell, the only thing they were thinking of was getting a little pussy. Ted had been waiting for this information. He finally knew all of those involved and what each person had done.   Now, it was time to implement his attack, and finally, get justice for Mack and Terry.

"What's wrong with you?" Rat had been carefully watching Ted the entire time while the others were reminiscing of the torture and murders of Mack and Terry.

"Is all this upsetting you?"   He leaned forward, looking Ted directly in the eyes.

"No, I don't care what happened to the fools. I'm just getting a little tired. It's late, and I've been up for nearly twenty-four hours." Ted had tried to hide his emotions, but he was not sure if he had been successful.

"He's right; it's getting late. We need to be fresh for tomorrow. We all know our parts, so there shouldn't be any surprises. Come on, let's go and relax for a while." Ron stood and walked to the door, which leads back to the main room with the rest of the group following behind him.

Ted was the last one to get up from the table. He knew what he had to do to fulfill his revenge.   He would not let them destroy another life the way they had with Mack and Terry.

A shiver of excitement came over him at the realization of the events to come.

Tonight, you will finally have your justice, Mack, and Terry. These assholes will pay for what they did, and pay with their blood.

Chapter 11

"Shit, Ron, I can't believe you left me out in the car!" Charlene yelled as she came in the door.

She had awakened to the loud banging sound of the trashcans when the city workers had come through on their nightly run. "Something could have happened to me out there!"

It had only been a month since Charlene had left her life in Fresno, a small rural community in central California. She had told her parents that she wanted to find universal truth and peace and to do her part to stop the war. Her parents had tried to get her to come back home, but she wanted to follow Ron after meeting him at an anti-war rally at Berkley.

"Maybe you should just shut the hell up and bring my pipe over here!" Ron hated her constant complaining, but she did have her uses, and he knew she would do anything he asked of her.

Stupid, mindless bitch, he thought to himself.

"It's time to relax before tomorrow," Ron said, letting Ted know to join him at one of the spindle tables.

"Yeah, that's a good idea!" Todd was beginning to come down from his high, and he did not like the feeling one bit. He flopped down on one of the mattresses and lit up a joint that was lying on the table, taking a deep drag on it.

"Shit, Todd, save some of that for us," Joel laughed as he sat down next to Todd.

"Never mind, I don't want any of that sissy shit; hash is the only way to go, man." Joel reached for one of the foil packets, opened it, then lifted the dark ball to his nose, and inhaled deeply. "Ah, now that's the shit, man."

Ted stood back, fighting the rage burning inside of him. *You need to control yourself. It will all be over soon.* He closed his eyes for a moment, trying to clear his mind.

"Come sit over here by me," Ron motioned to Ted, as he took his place on one of the mattresses lying next to one of the spindle tables.

"I have something that will help you relax."
He reached into his pocket and pulled out a
small vial, "Here, a little of this, and you'll
forget all your troubles."

Ted walked to the table and sat across from
Ron. He looked at the vial in Ron's hand.
"No, thanks, I'm not into that kind of shit. I
like to relax in my own way. I watched too
many men lose their minds on shit like that;
it's not my thing. Besides, I need to be clear-
headed for tomorrow."

Ron looked at Ted then smiled in
acknowledgment. "Hey, I can respect that.
You're right, but I hope you don't mind if I
partake of this magnificent substance." He
smiled with the anticipation of the amazing
time ahead.

"Not at all, enjoy yourself," Ted shrugged
his shoulders as he looked around the room at
the others. Tonight, is the night he had longed
for all those long months.

Charlene was sitting at one of the tables
with Ray, Steve, and another girl, and he
overheard Steve call the other girl, Willow.
*So, that's the other bitch. You both will pay
tonight for your treachery.*

As the evening went on, Ted was pleased
with the way things were developing. Tony

and Todd were so stoned that they had both passed out and were sleeping like a couple of babies on one of the mattresses. Rat and Ron were sitting together, tripping on the contents of the vial, while Ray, Steve, Charlene, and Willow were on one of the other mattresses sharing some opium-laced pot from a large multicolored bong.

Ted heard the girls giggling and make comments on how they wanted to have some real fun, so Steve reached for a bag on the table filled with magic mushrooms, and then fed them to each of the girls. "Here you go, ladies; this will help you enjoy the show."

Joel and Dean had been at the table with the weapons going over the inventory for nearly an hour when Ron motioned for them to come and join the group. "You two will get to play with those soon enough, come on; it's time to relax and enjoy."

"He's right; I could use a little release," Joel chuckled as he walked to the table where Ron, Rat, and Ted were sitting. He sat down and then moved over to let Dean sit next to him.

Once he was comfortable, he reached for the vial in Ron's outstretched hand, "Man, tomorrow is going to be great!"

"It sure is," Dean laughed. "I can't wait to watch that baby killer burn!"

***

Another hour had passed, as Ted waited to act. The room was quiet now, as everyone was either asleep or so strung out that none of them had no idea what was going on around them. Ted had kept his eyes closed to make it appear as though he was asleep, but he was actually waiting for the proper time to strike.

Shit, this is going to be like killing fish in a barrel, he silently laughed to himself.

He finally opened his eyes, careful not to move as he looked around the room. Tony and Todd had passed out on the mattress to the left of him, and Ray, Steve, Charlene, and Willow were all lying in one big heap; out to the world.

Joel and Dean were sitting back, enjoying their high with Ron and Rat.

Just a little bit longer, Ted thought to himself.

Chapter 12

Ted lay there for what seemed like an eternity and waited until silence filled the room. He slowly opened his eyes and glanced around the room.

Good, now it's finally time for justice, he thought to himself as he felt the adrenaline surge through his body.

The vision in his mind of what was to happen next gave Ted great satisfaction, it also made his senses sharpen to the point where everything was crystal clear around him.

Everyone in the room was now sleeping, except for Ted. While he was waiting, he had gone over in his mind what he was going to do. As for Tony and Todd, he had no plan to kill them. They were just a couple of fools who were more interested in getting stoned than hurting anyone.

The girls were a different matter altogether. They had lured Terry and Mack to their deaths, and for that, they would pay. Ted had decided not to kill them, as he knew they were simply foolish girls caught up in something they did not fully understand. However, they would pay for their part in all of this, and pay dearly.

Then there was Ron and Rat. Neither of them was directly involved in the killings, but they did plan and sanction it, so for that, they would also pay.

Now, as far as Ray, Steve, Dean, and Joel, Ted had special plans for them. They would know the pain they had inflicted on Mack and Terry and would die with full knowledge of the agony and terror each one endured.

Ted had a clear image in his mind of each participant in his plan for justice, this causing a smile to appear on his face.

Time to begin, he thought to himself.

***

It was all too easy. Tony and Todd had slept while Ted dragged their mattress into the back room, closed the door, and locked them inside. Charlene and Willow were so out of it that they did not notice when Ted placed them in chairs next to each other in the center of the room. Neither girl even flinched when he bound and gagged them.

Things were a little tricky for the rest of the group, as Ted wanted no mistakes with them. He pulled a small bottle of ether from his pocket and dampened a handkerchief with it. Then one by one, Ted pressed it over the nose and mouth of the rest of the sleeping group, ensuring they would not wake up until he was ready for them. Once he knew each one was unconscious, he began his plan.

"Now, you will finally receive your justice, Terry, and Mack," Ted said to himself, with the vision of the night's coming events forming in his mind.

***

The room was eerily dark except for one lone bulb shining down in the center of the room. The scene playing out in the room was like that of a torture chamber from an old horror movie. Ray, Joel, Steve, and Dean hung side-by-side, nude, and by their upstretched arms from the ceiling rafters.

Bound, gagged, and sitting on either side of the hanging group were Ron and Rat. Lastly, were Willow and Charlene, poised, and sitting in chairs facing the men as if they were two spectators at a sick and twisted theater show.

Ted stepped back and surveyed the scene one last time. Once he saw there was nothing more to prepare, he said to the unconscious group, "Perfection; let's begin."

***

WHAM! The sound of fist on flesh stirred the group to consciousness just in time to see blood spray from Rat's nose.

"To have served and come back to the world only to celebrate the destruction of your brothers makes me sick! I have something very special planned for you, something only you will understand." Ted leaned forward, forcing Rat to look him directly in the eyes.

Ted then stepped back to watch the look of acknowledgment on Rat's face. "But first, I want you to enjoy the show I have planned. It will be very entertaining, I promise you."

Ted grinned as he saw a look of dread suddenly appear in Rat's eyes. "So, why don't we get started?"

Ted turned and walked to the middle of the group, where he stopped to survey the scene before him. The terror was thick in the air, and it wrapped around him like a warm blanket. He took his time to look at each set of eyes, and thoroughly enjoyed the look of horror and fear he saw in them.

No, I'm not going to rush things; this is going to last long enough to avenge the suffering that Mack and Terry both endured.

"I'm sure you are all wondering what has brought us to this little situation tonight," Ted asked in a playful tone.

"Well, you see, you all have a debt to repay." He took his time, looking at each one, clearly seeing the puzzled look in their eyes.

"Oh, that's right, you have no idea what I'm talking about, do you? Well, let me shed some light on things."

Ted had waited for this moment for months. To face the scum who had murdered Mack, and Terry was one of the most satisfying feelings he had ever known. He briefly closed his eyes, remembering the promise he had made to Mr. Smitten, wishing that he could know that Mack and Terry would finally receive justice for their deaths.

Ted then opened his eyes and drew in a deep breath before he spoke, "Several months ago, three young soldiers returned home from the war wanting nothing more than to restart their lives. The only thing they wanted was to have a little fun before returning to their families and the lives they had left behind to serve their country."

Ted paused a moment to watch the realization begin to form in their eyes.

"Then, on a beautiful, sun-filled morning, two of them decided to leave their hotel room to explore the city. They had hoped to find a couple of friendly, young ladies to spend some time with, and as luck would have it, they did."

Ted turned and looked directly at Willow and Charlene. "The girls they found were the two of you."

Willow and Charlene both looked into his eyes and saw the rage burning there. "You both knew a couple of guys back from the war would be looking for the company of two friendly girls such as yourselves, didn't you? You led them to that alley, and then distracted them by sucking their cocks!"

Ted leaned in closer and looked directly into their tear-filled eyes and softly said, "You led them to the slaughter, and you did it willingly."

The tears flowed from their eyes at the understanding of his words. They tried to speak but were unable with the tape placed tightly across their mouths.

Once Ted saw the understanding in their eyes, he continued. "So, you do remember?"

Both girls nodded in unison.

That's good, and there's no need for tears because you won't be dying today. The only thing you two need to do is sit back and enjoy the show."

He slid his hand into his jacket pocket, pulled out a small vial with an eyedropper, and held it up so both girls could clearly see.

"I hope you like this special treat I have for you, ladies. I'm sure Ron won't mind if you have some, and since you're both a little tied up at the moment, I'll help you." He opened the vial, inserted the eyedropper, and pulled in the liquid.

"I'm sure you both will love the effects of this, so just sit back and have an enjoyable time. Here you go, Charlene; you first."

Ted reached for Charlene as she fought to turn her head away from him. "Now, now, don't fight it. In a few moments, you'll be having an enjoyable time. Just a little in each eye ought to do the trick."

He grasped her eyelid with his thumb and held her eye open while he emptied half of the contents from the eyedropper, and then he did the same in her other eye.

"There you go. You will be feeling much better in no time."

He released her, and then returned the eyedropper to the vial. "Now, it's Willows turn."

He repeated the process on Willow, then once he was done, he stepped back.

"Oh, yes, I almost forgot something. We wouldn't want the two of you not to enjoy the entire show, now would we?"

Ted snickered as he reached for the two small pieces of tape he had stuck to her chair while she was unconscious.

"I wouldn't want you two to close your eyes and miss all the fun," he laughed, as he placed a piece of tape on each eyelid to force their eyes to stay open.

"There you go; that's better. I hope you enjoy the show I have planned for you, I'm sure it will be quite entertaining."

He leaned in closer and saw pleasure dancing in his eyes. "Ah yes, you're both beginning to feel much better now, aren't you?"

***

Ted stood in the middle of the group, relishing the moment. He had waited for this day, and he fully intended to see that each one of them paid for their part in the murders of Mack and Terry.

He closed his eyes to the vision of Terry's father lying in the hospital bed, with his words playing again in his mind. *They need to pay, Ted. They can't destroy lives like that, and not pay.*

Ted felt his blood surging through his veins with a renewed sense of purpose. *Don't worry, Mr. Smitten; they'll pay for their evil deed, and they'll pay today.*

With the vision still clearly etched in his mind, Ted turned to face the rest of the group.

Chapter 13

Ted paused and then looked at each of the men hanging before him. He fully enjoyed the look of fear in their eyes, as well as the muffled cries from behind their taped mouths. He took his time to look at each one in the eyes while he enjoyed seeing their growing fear.

"This is going to be the day you will all repay the debt you owe. Justice will finally be served." Ted watched the fear in their eyes transform into one of terror.

Ted turned and walked toward Ron first, and stopped a few feet away from him. "Don't worry; you're not going to die right now. I want you to enjoy the show along with the girls. However, you will not be getting any of the special stuff as they did. I want you to see everything I do to those four over there. I want you to watch everything they will endure as they die. I want you to understand what those two soldiers went through when your friends tortured them to death. No, you will not miss a thing; I'll make sure of it."

With that last statement, Ted reached for the two small pieces of tape he had placed on the back of the chair. He then smiled as he put them on Ron's eyelids to hold his eyes open, as he had done to the girls.

Once the tape was in place, he leaned in close to Ron and whispered in his ear, "And once they're dead, you will die. See, you have to cut the head off the snake to make sure it's dead. For this reason, once you're dead, your little group will be gone forever. You will no longer be able to recruit fools to kill unsuspecting soldiers who only want to reclaim their lives. So, sit here and enjoy the show. Look, the girls already are having an excellent time."

He grasped Ron's head, forcing it to turn toward Willow and Charlene, who were already under the influence of the drug he had given them.

"See, they appear to be having a wonderful trip, but I'm sure this will be one they will not want to return from."

Ted released Ron's head and walked over to face the four hanging in the center of the room. He stood silently for a few moments, taking in the scene before him.

"Not so tough now, are you?" Ted chuckled with sarcasm dripping from every word. He leaned down and pulled his hunting knife from his pack sitting on the floor.

"Let's see here, I do believe it was Joel who bragged about how much fun it was skinning the two baby killers, wasn't it? You know, when I was a child, my mother would take me and my brother to church every Sunday. We'd sit and listen to the preacher talk about how in the Old Testament it said that you must pay for your sins in the old way: an eye for an eye. Yep, I do believe that's just what that old preacher said was in the Bible. You know, my mama would be disappointed in me if I didn't do what that old preacher said," Ted grinned at seeing the look of fear in their eyes.

Ted walked up to Joel with their eyes meeting. Joel understood what Ted meant, but he did not want to give Ted the satisfaction of knowing the fear that was building up inside of him. His body went rigid as he tried to prepare himself for what he knew was about to come.

Ted saw the look of defiance in Joel's eyes. "So, you're not afraid? Good, it will make this much easier. I want to let you know that I have had a lot of experience with skinning hogs back home, so I'm quite good with a knife. I saw, by your handy work, that you've never skinned anything before. You were quite sloppy, but you won't have to worry about that with me. I know what to do, and I promise that you'll not die right away either. You see, I want to be sure that you have plenty of time to comprehend the pain you caused."

Ted looked him in the eye and smiled as he pressed the razor-sharp knife against the tender skin of Joel's inner right thigh, causing the blood to flow onto the blade. "Let's get started."

***

Twenty minutes had passed since Ted began working on Joel. Once he finished, he stepped back to view his handy work, but what hung there no longer resembled a human being. The skin from the neck down now lay on the floor next to the stripped feet barely touching the bloody floor.

Ted had left the skin on the skull; however, he had removed each cyclid to expose his terror-filled eyes. Ted wanted to make sure

Joel would watch everything that was happening to the others while he died.

Ted wiped the blood from the blade of his knife and slid it back between his belt and jeans. He then looked into Joel's lidless eyes and calmly said, "Now you know the pain you inflicted, and once you finally die, your debt will be paid."

Ted then turned and walked over to face Dean and Ray, who were hanging beside each other. He leaned in closely, looking at both of them before he spoke. "You both thought it was funny to cut off their penises and shove them into the other one's mouth, didn't you? Well, you will have the same done to you except for one slight difference."

He turned to face Dean, and with one clean swipe of his knife, he now held the severed member in his hand. The tape placed securely across his mouth, muffled the screams of agony, but the pain was evident in his eyes.

Ted lifted his hand, allowing Dean to see the blood-covered penis, which was no longer a part of his body and smiled.

Their eyes never broke contact as he reached into his back pocket and pulled out a short, round, metal rod. Firmly holding the bloody penis, he forced the rod into it.

"Let's see how Ray feels about you fucking him while he dies," Ted chuckled, as he walked around behind Ray, who was desperately fighting to free himself.

Once Ted stood behind Ray, he placed the tip of the penis against the unwelcoming opening and rammed it in as far as it would go.

Muffled screams erupted from behind the tape as Ray struggled to free himself, but to no avail. Ted then leaned forward and whispered into Ray's ear, "I hope it was as good for you, as it was for me. Now it's your turn to return the favor."

Ted walked around to face Ray, whose eyes were wild with fear, and tears streamed down his cheeks. Without saying a word, Ted merely smiled, and again with one clean swipe, he held the severed member in his hand.

He then turned to face Dean, who was now growing ashen from the loss of blood, and calmly said, "Your turn."

He reached into the same back pocket, pulled out another metal rod, and forced it into the severed penis. Ted then walked around behind Dean and rammed the penis and rod as deeply as the first one.

Once done, he leaned forward and whispered in Dean's ear, "Now everyone will know the truth about you two, won't they?"

Ted stepped back to face the group, enjoying the vision before him. He then turned to look at the two girls, still bound in the chairs with a look of terror in their eyes, and said teasingly, "Are you enjoying the show, ladies?"

The smell of blood was thick in the air, almost as thick as the fear and pain. Ted walked over to face Steve, who was nearly insane with fear.

"I bet you're wondering why I saved you for last. It wasn't because you did the worst, or because I was not going to do anything to you. It was because I wanted you to see and hear everything I did to your friends. Don't worry; you'll get to repay your debt," Ted grinned.

"You bragged of gouging out their eyes and burning off their ears. Then you said how you laughed as you watched them fall to the ground. However, before we get to that, we need to write a little message just like you did. I want the world to know what you are." Without another word, Ted took his knife, placed it on Steve's chest, and with each slice carved the word *COWARD* so deeply that he cut into bone.

Once he finished, Ted stepped back to view his handiwork. "That will do nicely. Now let's take care of the rest," Ted chuckled as he reached into his pocket and pulled out a Zippo cigarette lighter and a small can of Ronson lighter fluid.

As he held the items for Steve to see, a look of terror filled his eyes at the realization of what was to come.

"Shall we begin?" Ted smiled as he opened the container of fluid and thoroughly soaked each ear.

The overpowering smell of the lighter fluid filled the air, as Steve struggled to free himself from this nightmare. He closed his eyes and prayed for an escape from this horror; however, the sound of the lid as it flipped open, made it clear that it was time to face his punishment.

Ted enjoyed the look of fear on Steve's face. He wanted him to understand the same pain that Mack and Terry had endured at his hands. He firmly held the lighter, and then spun the wheel, thus causing the flint to spark and ignite the wick.

As he paused for a moment, Ted remembered the first day of his friendship with Mack and Terry. It was the day the sniper had attacked their unit. Once things had calmed down, Ted pulled a cigarette from his pocket and was about to light it when Mack walked up to him.

"Hey, you wouldn't have another one of those, would you?" Mack asked with a nervous smile on his face.

"Sure, take this one," Ted laughed. *He then handed the cigarette to Mack and reached into his pocket for another one.*

"I wouldn't mind one of those if you can spare another one," Terry smiled as he sat next to Ted on a fallen tree. *"Man, you saved our butts back there."*

"You sure did," Mack laughed. *"I thought I was going home in a body bag for sure."*

"He's right. We're lucky that all of us aren't dead," Terry said, as took the offered cigarette.

Ted lit his cigarette and then held the lighter out for Mack to light his.

"Thanks," Mack said after taking a long pull on it.

"Do you mind if I have a light before you put that away?" Terry asked.

Ted looked at Terry and nodded his acknowledgment, but instead of holding the flame in place for Terry, he closed the lid to the lighter.

"Why did you do that?" Terry asked.

Ted did not say a word; he simply flipped the lid on the lighter and ignited the flame, and then held it in place for Terry.

Terry looked at Ted, unsure of what to think. After a few tense moments, he leaned forward and then pulled a deep drag on the cigarette. "Thanks."

"Okay, why did you do that?" Mack laughed.

"Yeah, why did you restart the lighter?" Terry smiled as he took another long drag on his cigarette.

Ted had put the lighter back in his pocket before he spoke, "Three on a match."

Mack and Terry looked at each other, unsure of what they had heard.

"Three on a match, what does that mean?" Terry asked.

"You two must be greenhorns," Ted laughed. "It's from World War One. You see, there was a belief that if three soldiers lit their cigarettes from the same match, one of the three would be killed or that the man who was

third on the match would be shot. You see, the first one gives the enemy marksman the range to the target, the second one gives the windage on the target, and finally, the third one is shot using this all of this information." He smiled at seeing the surprised looks on their faces. "After our little run-in today, I don't believe that any of us wants to take the chance."

"Oh, I get it. Since you restarted the flame, it was not three men on one match, or, in this case, one flame. Am I correct?" Mack smiled.

Ted looked and Mack and smiled, "that's right."

Terry began to laugh, "Damn, I think we need to stick with you for the rest of our time here. I don't know about Cowboy here, but I'd like to go home in one piece and still be breathing."

Mack nodded in agreement. "Joker's right. We need to stick with someone who can save our sorry asses.

"Your name is Ted, isn't it?" Terry asked.

"Yes," Ted said flatly.

"No, I think his name should be The Executioner," Mack laughed.

"The Executioner, I like that. It's perfect. He's just the guy we need to take care of the bad guys," Terry grinned.

***

"It's fitting that I use this lighter on a piece of shit like you. You thought it was funny to burn the ears off my friends. You laughed at the pain they endured, and now you will know that same pain," Ted smiled as he rubbed his thumb on the wheel, causing it to spin and ignite the flame.

The site of the flames dancing before him caused Steve to feel faint. He knew what was ahead for him, and there was nothing he could do to prevent it from happening.

Ted watched the flame flickering in the dim light of the room, as he slowly lifted it to the first liquid-soaked ear. The fluid instantly burst into flames, burning with such intensity that it caused his hair to burst into flames. Ted then put the flame to the other ear, causing the same effect. The look of agony was clearly in Steve's eyes, but no one could hear his muffled cries for mercy.

Ted leaned in and looked Steve directly eyes, and said with a chill in his voice, "I want my face to be the last thing you see before you die. I want your last memory to be of how I destroyed you and your friends. I want you to die with the knowledge that your death is the payment for the murder of two of the best people I've ever known."

Ted paused a moment before he took his knife and reached for the first terror-filled eye.

***

The feelings of pleasure washed over Ted like waves on a beach. He turned to look once more at the scene in the middle of the room, and the four figures hanging there as if out of a nightmare. Each was limp and lifeless, with only an occasional involuntary twitch from a pain-filled muscle. A soft whimpering filled the room, and Ted took a deep breath, enjoying the vision before him.

"Several months ago, on a beautiful sun-filled day, my two best friends only wanted to reclaim their lives. Both had survived the war and then came home merely to be murdered because they were soldiers. You thought it was funny to strike them down with no more feeling that you would give a bug on the wall. You all bragged about the fun you had with Mack and Terry, and how much you enjoyed watching them die in the most painful and demeaning way. Today the debt you owed is paid in full, and I hope you enjoy your eternity in hell," Ted said to the group before he turned to face Ron and Rat.

He stood a moment, enjoying the look of fear in their eyes before he finally spoke, "Okay, now it's time to take care of you two. Let's start with you, Ron. I plan to save Rat for the last. Besides, I've been looking forward to our time together."

***

Ted slowly walked around Ron and Rat, gently touching them on the top of the head as he passed by. He stopped behind Ron, whispering into his ear, "Not so brave now, are you? I bet you never thought of how your victims would feel when you planned your attacks on them, did you? So, how does it feel to be on the other side now? You've enjoyed being the leader of this group of terrorists and the head of the snake. Well, in Texas, we have a saying; the best way to kill a snake is to cut off its head. So, I would be remiss, not to follow that good, old tradition."

Ted paused a moment before pulling wire with two small pieces of wood attached to either end out of his pocket. Then before Ron knew what was happening, Ted wrapped the wire around Ron's neck and removed his head with one motion from his body.

Ted grasped the long hair, lifting the disembodied head, and then turned it to face him. The look of shock and horror was clearly in the wide-open eyes. Ted smiled as he looked into the face of death, and then laughed as he noticed how Ron's mouth was slowly moving from behind the tape as though trying to make a silent protest.

"Now I don't have to worry about you starting up another group of cowards. Your days of planning against this country are over," Ted chuckled.

He walked around to the front of Ron's body, securely tied to the chair. Ted smiled, and then he turned the head toward the beheaded body, as the last of the blood gushed from the neck like a water fountain with each beat of his dying heart.

"Now your debt is finally paid," he said with a sense of satisfaction, as he placed the severed head on the lap of the dead body.

Ted took a few steps back, closed his eyes, and drew in a deep breath. A feeling of warmth and contentment washed over him, but he knew he still had one last thing to do.

With that thought, he opened his eyes and turned to face Rat. "Well, I guess it's just you and me now."

***

The look in Rats eyes was one of defiance and hate. Ted smiled and walked to a table in the back of the room without saying a word. He picked up a small box and burlap bag and then walked back over to where Rat was sitting.

"I bet you're wondering what I have planned for you? I know you've probably heard of this deadly torture the Vietcong did to American Soldiers over there; so, I felt it only fitting for a traitor such as yourself."

Ted stopped in front of Rat and shook the box. The sounds now emanating from the box brought fear to Rat's eyes.

"Ah, so you have heard of this? I remember the first time I saw the effect of this little contraption. My unit had just returned to base after several days out on patrol to quite a bit of commotion. You see, the night before our return, a couple of new grunts decided not to follow orders. They got a little too comfortable and fell asleep during their guard duty. The poor bastards never knew what hit them until it was too late." Ted paused a moment to enjoy the look of recognition in Rat's eyes.

"It really was quite tragic. The first one was found dead after having bashed in his brains while trying to kill the attackers. Most of his face was gone; hell, he didn't even look human anymore. Damn, if he didn't break his own skull wide open before he was able to kill them. The second one was not as lucky. He survived, though just barely. I know you must remember the size of those rats over there, don't you? The damn things are the size of an ordinary alley cat, and ten times as mean," Ted grinned at seeing the tears form in Rat's eyes.

"The second grunt had finally killed the two attackers, but not before, they had eaten his nose, both ears, one of his eyes, and most of his tongue. Hell, it would have been better for him if he'd died as the other poor fool. He'd crushed most of the bones in his face while he beat the two rats to death. The doctors said if he survived his injuries, he would probably spend the rest of his life in an institution for the mentally insane. Yeah, it would have been better for him if he'd died like the other one."

Ted shook the box again, causing the contents inside to protest. "I'm sorry I wasn't able to find some as large as the ones in Vietnam, so I figured it would take a few extra to achieve the same effect. It wasn't hard to find them since this place is over-run with them. I think six should do just fine. What do you say?"

Ted shook the box again, causing the protests to be louder than before.

Rat could no longer control his fear as he fully understood what was about to happen to him. He had heard of this being done to unsuspecting soldiers in Vietnam, and the very thought of it made his stomach turn. He tried to compose himself for what was about to happen, but he failed.

Ted fully enjoyed the look he saw in those fear-filled eyes. "Well, I guess we might as well get started."

He walked up to Rat and ripped the tape off his mouth, causing wails of rage to fly from him.

"You bastard, I'm going to kill you!" Rat yelled while he fought to free himself.

Ted smiled, and calmly replied, "You are? I have to admit that I like your spirit. I was hoping you wouldn't go out as a coward like the rest of them."

Rat looked directly at him and said in a low voice, "Just let me go, and I'll show you some fucking spirit." Rage and fear now consumed him.

This reaction, of course, pleased Ted. He shook his head and replied in a teasing manner, "I would like to, but that would screw with my plans for you. You see, we wouldn't want to do that, now would we? I bet you're wondering why I pulled the tape off your mouth. I didn't want you to miss the sound of your screams, as these little guys do their work. I know I'm looking forward to listening, as they get to know you. Well, I guess we might as well get started with the fun."

Ted walked around behind Rat and placed the burlap bag over the top of the box. He then carefully lifted the box to pour the protesting contents into the bag. Once they were in the bottom of the bag, he quickly closed his hand around the opening to hold back the angry group as they tried to escape.

"Boy, they sure sound pissed, don't they? Ah, well, in a few seconds they'll have something new to focus on," a soft laugh escaped his lips.

Rat closed his eyes while tears flowed down his cheeks and awaited his fate.

***

Ted lifted the opening over Rat's head and then carefully put his head inside while his other hand secured the angry group at the bottom of the bag. Once he had Rats head completely inside, and twine tightly secured around his neck, he released the attackers.

The screams were immediate and intense, as Ted stepped back to take inventory of the scene.

Rat tried to rock the chair to make it fall over. He then attempted to push back with his feet, but it did not work because Ted had taped his ankles to the front legs of the chair. He shook his head from side to side, trying to keep the painful attackers from his bleeding head, but nothing would stop them.

The pain now was overwhelming, as the ripping of razor-like teeth was beyond anything he could ever have imagined. One of the rats that had been chewing on his bottom lip was now working on the inside of his mouth, ripping small pieces of soft flesh.

Another one had pulled the eyelashes from his left eyelid and was now licking at the tears and blood as it pooled in the corner of the eye and bridge of his nose. He could feel the scratches across his face from their needle-sharp claws, and on his scalp.

This was more than Rat could handle, as a rush of adrenaline surged through his body. "I have to end this. I can't take this any longer!" He screamed, then he slipped into a dark place of swirling insanity.

Ted stepped around in front of Rat to get a full view of the scene as it played out before him. The screams still came from inside the burlap bag, but they seemed slightly garbled now.

He turned to look at the two women still sitting there. "Are you girls enjoying the show?" he laughed.

"Hell, I might as well sit down and enjoy it with you." He walked to a chair that was sitting nearby and carried it over to sit next to Charlotte.

"I hope you're both enjoying this as much as I am. Ah, you two don't look so well; what's wrong, not having any fun?" he teased.

"What's the matter, Willow? I thought you two liked this sort of thing. Well, I guess neither of you really know how to have fun." Ted looked at the two of them closer, noticing the look of insanity in their eyes.

"Well, I'll be damned, it appears the two of you have already left the show; what a shame." He leaned back in his chair and clasped his hands behind his head.

"Oh well, I guess I'll just have to enjoy it all by myself."

***

As Ted sat there, a feeling of peace flowed over him. He closed his eyes, and a vision of Mack and Terry appeared in his mind. They each stood in front of him, with the same bright smiles he had seen so many times before.

Ted's heart raced at the sight of them. *Guys, this won't happen to anyone else, I promise you. I'll make sure your deaths were not in vain. Whenever there's someone who decides to harm the innocent and then manages to beat the system, I'll be there to make sure payment is made for the debt owed. No longer will victims and their families be ignored by the courts and never know justice for the atrocities committed against them. If this country is going to allow the guilty to walk free, then I'll make it my mission to see they pay for their deeds. I love you guys, and I'm sorry I wasn't there to help you.*

He paused a moment, not wanting the vision to go away. *Terry, let your father know that I kept my promise, and Mack, I'm sorry we never got to go on that hunting trip. I want you both to know it was an honor and pleasure serving with you, as well as calling you, my friends. I will never forget you.*

As Ted sat quietly, the vision of Mack and Terry slowly began to fade from his mind. He then heard these words float softly into his mind, *Thank you, you will always be our friend.*

Chapter 14

Present Day

"Oh, God, please, no!" Doug cried out as he sat up in bed with his body trembling and covered in sweat.

Detective Doug Mabry hated to sleep as the memory of his wife and daughter's horrible deaths invaded his dreams. It was seventeen years since they had been murdered while Doug served in the Middle East during the first Gulf War. It was a day that the unthinkable happened and changed his life forever.

***

Doug and Donna had been in the foster child system for most of their childhood. They had met when placed in the same home for a few months at the age of nine and had become best friends until Doug moved to another home.

They had lost touch until one day when they were in high school and saw each other in the line at the local movie theater. They were surprised to learn that they had been living only a few miles apart for the past couple of years, and from that day forward, they were inseparable. The day they both turned eighteen and were free from the system, they began to plan their lives together as husband and wife.

Doug had never liked school, so college was never in his plans. He knew life would be difficult without a skill, which is why he decided serving in the military would be the best way to provide for his family and to do something of value.

Doug was tired of feeling as if he was nothing; the way he had while in the foster care system. His mother had been a runaway who had died during childbirth, and no one knew of his father. The authorities had tried in vain to find any living relatives, but after several attempts, they had given up.

The only world he knew as a child was the constant moving from one foster home to another, never knowing what it felt like to belong to a family.

The same was true for Donna. She had been five years old when she entered the system. Her mother had started drinking when her father committed suicide, making for a very rough life for Donna. Starting from the tender age of three years old, her mother would leave her alone for hours while she was out at the local bars, drinking and selling herself to make money.

Then one night, when the apartment building they lived in had caught fire, it was only by accident that a firefighter found her huddled in the corner of the kitchen. Taken from her mother after the fire, the authorities placed Donna in the foster care system. Donna's distraught mother then committed suicide at losing Donna, leaving her all alone with no known family members.

A strong bond had formed between Doug and Donna because they each understood what it was to be alone. However, Doug knew it would break her heart when he told her of his decision to join the military because he would be away from her for long periods while serving.

For this reason, on the day he decided to tell her his decision, he braced himself for the worst. She surprised him, though, by calmly saying she understood and would support him in whatever he thought was best. They decided to get married before he enlisted, so after a small civil ceremony, he headed straight to the recruiting office to enlist.

The next three years were the happiest years of Doug's life. He had married the love of his life and was proudly serving in the Marines at Camp Pendleton in Southern California. Doug had plans for his military career, so he worked hard to complete the necessary qualifications for training in the Special Forces. Then on the day he received the news that he was chosen, it was the proudest day of his life. Not only had he achieved the ultimate dream of his military career thus far, but also, Donna had told him that he was going to be a father. His life was now complete.

Doug was beside himself with joy. He had a loving wife, a fulfilling career, and soon he would have a family of his own. Things were finally going his way for the first time in his life; however, life sometimes has other plans for us.

***

The excitement around the base was evident by the smiles on the faces of the men. Finally, all their training and hard work would be put to the test. Saddam Hussein had invaded Kuwait, so the United States, along with the

United Kingdom and thirty-four other countries had joined together, forming a coalition force to push Hussein's army back to Iraq. The day Doug received his orders made for a mixture of emotions. He was excited about the opportunity to serve his country by defeating an invading force. However, he was also sad because he would miss the birth of his first child. Donna was now in her seventh month and getting bigger with each passing day.

They both were excited the first time the baby had kicked Doug's hand while he was caressing Donna's stomach.

"Man, this one is going to be a football kicker, I know it!" Doug laughed, rubbing her tummy, and trying to find the little foot again.

The thought of not being with Donna for the last part of the pregnancy tore at his heart, but she assured him that she and the baby would be okay.

She had told him, "You need to focus on your job. Go over there, kick some butt, and then come home safely to us. Honey, I'm so proud of you, and I don't want you to worry because we'll both be here waiting for you to come home."

The time had passed quickly, and before he knew it, he was shipped out along with the rest of his unit.

***

Doug was glad they were busy, as it helped the time pass. He was also glad whenever he was able to talk Donna because, with the work he was doing, Doug did not get to stay in contact with her as much as he would have liked.

The news of the birth of his first child was the happiest day of Doug's life. Donna had gone through several long hours of labor, but in the end, she had delivered a beautiful and healthy baby girl.

Donna had told him that she decided to name her Miranda Louise Mabry, and he anxiously waited for the day when he would return home to meet his little girl for the first time.

The next few weeks flew by for Doug. The mission was going as planned, and he was pleased that Donna and little Miranda were doing fine. She had sent him several pictures, which he had proudly put up all on his side of the tent.

The other men loved to tease him, "That beautiful, little baby can't be yours because you're too damn ugly to be her daddy!" All the teasing never mattered to Doug. He would only smile and pray that the day of his homecoming would be soon.

Doug would never forget the day when his unit returned to base from being out on patrol. He had received news from home that would forever change his life.

His commander had called him in for a meeting, and by the look on his face, Doug knew it was not going to be good news. The words sunk into Doug's mind like a ship sailing into a fog bank, and no matter how hard he tried to make sense of them, he could not as they were too horrible to imagine.

"Sir, you must be mistaken. I spoke with her a few days ago. She's fine. You've been told this in error, Sir."

"I'm sorry, Son, I wish this were a mistake, but it's not. Yesterday evening, as your wife was leaving the parking lot of the local mall a man strung out on drugs attacked her and demanded money," Col. Bradshaw paused a moment before he continued.

"Witnesses say that he jumped into the car as she stopped at the light while leaving the mall, brandishing a handgun and ordering her to go to the ATM in the parking lot. Witnesses then said they heard her say that she would do whatever he wanted, as long as he did not harm her or her baby. Unfortunately, the baby began to cry, and this upset the attacker. He started to scream, *Get it to shut the fuck up, or I'll kill it!*"

Col. Bradshaw had never delivered this type of news to a soldier under him, and he prayed he would never have to again. In the past, he had given the sad news of a passing grandparent or parent, but this was by far the worst thing he ever had the unfortunate duty to do.

He steadied himself before continuing, "But before your wife could do anything, the bastard turned around and shot the baby."

At hearing the words, Doug fell to his knees, "Oh, God…no, not Miranda!"

The tears streamed down Doug's face, his heart feeling as though someone had kicked him in the chest. Suddenly, a thought came into his pained mind.

"What about Donna? Is she alright?" He looked up, his eyes pleading.

Col. Bradshaw swallowed hard and continued. "I'm sorry, Son; no, she's not.

When she realized what he had done, she attacked him. They wrestled over the gun, and she was shot and killed. By this time, the police were on the scene and had the car surrounded."

Col. Bradshaw's emotions overwhelmed him. He felt tears forming in the corners of his eyes, and his voice grew raspy.

"Damn it, son, your baby was still alive, and the sick bastard wouldn't let her go! He kept screaming that he had a baby in the car, and he wanted to be let go, or the baby would die. Witnesses said they could hear the soft cries coming from the backseat of the car…but…shit, he just sat there and was going to let her die!"

Col. Bradshaw could no longer hold back his tears. He closed his eyes and saw the smiling face of his first granddaughter in his mind that had just turned two years old the prior week. He could not imagine the depth of pain he would feel to have someone do that to his sweet, little angel.

Doug felt his life force torn from his soul. This all had to be a nightmare, and he prayed that he would awaken. However, he knew by the look on Col. Bradshaw's face that it was all true.

"What happened to the bastard who did this?" Doug asked, with the rage and pain growing inside of him to a dangerous level.

"Well, he proved to be an even greater coward. Once the police realized the baby was still alive in the backseat, they told him to gave himself up and help his case, but if he didn't, he could expect to spend the rest of his life locked up. He must not have liked the prospect of spending the rest of his life in prison as he jumped out of the car, screaming and firing his gun at the nearest squad car. Of course, it was only a matter of seconds before he was lying face down on the ground, wounded, but still breathing. I understand he's under arrest in the county hospital and facing double murder charges."

Col. Bradshaw paused for a few moments, and then took a deep breath as he tried to steady himself.

"Your daughter was a fighter. She made it to the hospital...," his voice cracked. "But she didn't have the strength to make it through the surgery. I'm so sorry."

With these last words, Doug felt his will to live vanish. How could his life have taken such a turn?

"Sir, I don't know what to do…" his words trailed off, as he was unable to form anymore.

Col. Bradshaw looked into Doug's pain-filled eyes and wished he knew what to say to make this all go away.

"Son, I've already made the necessary arrangements for you to return stateside today. I know you have arrangements to make for your family, and you need to be there. You will let me know of anything that I can do for you, right? We are your brothers, so never forget that."

Doug looked at Col. Bradshaw with tears and pain clearly in his eyes. "Thank you, Sir. Thank you for being honest with me about what happened."

He brought his hand up to salute. Col. Bradshaw stood, returned the salute, and then said, "I thought you deserved nothing less than the complete truth, Son. Now get going, you don't want to miss your flight."

Doug stood in place as he looked into the eyes of a man that he had always respected and genuinely liked. "Yes, sir!"

With those words, Doug turned and left the command tent, and headed to gather his things for the long flight back home.

Chapter 15

The flight back to the states seemed to drag on forever. Doug had hoped he could just sleep the whole time, but dreams of Donna and Miranda lying there dead before him was something he did not want to endure.

Once he arrived home, he had planned to head straight to the coroner's office to claim Donna and Miranda's bodies for burial. When he reached the base, he was thankful when Donna's best friend, Stacy Mitchell, had shown up to give him a ride.

Stacy and Donna had both been pregnant at the same time. With this being Stacy's third child, she had been a great help and support to Donna through the months while Doug was away.

Stacy had been the one to go and identify the bodies. She was a strong woman, having grown up on Marine bases, but then, of course, she had fallen in love with and married a Marine. Donna had said that she would never have made it through the hours of labor without Stacy there to keep her in line.

"Toughen up, girl; this is no time to be weak!" Stacy had barked at her the entire time.

Donna laughed as she told Doug how she had felt as if she was in boot camp, not a delivery room. Donna always said that Stacy was like the big sister she had always wanted, but today Stacy did not look so tough. Her eyes were red, and she carried herself with a sadness Doug had never seen in her before.

During the drive to the coroner's office, neither of them had spoken a word, but once they pulled up the driveway, Stacy broke the silence.

"Doug, I've already started the arrangements for the funeral home, I hope you don't mind? Several of us got together and raised the money for a beautiful headstone for them. You only need to let us know what you want to put on it."

The look on his face let her know he was thankful but was not ready to talk about it yet.

"Oh shit, I'm sorry. I can be such an ass at times, I'm sorry," her cheeks turned a dark red at the choice of her words. She did not say another word as she pulled up in front of the door and parked.

"No, I'm sorry, Stacy. You've done more than anyone could ever expect. You have been a wonderful friend to Donna, and I want to thank you for everything you did to help her. I appreciate your help more than you will ever know, but I have to take care of this before I can think of anything else." Doug opened the door and stepped out of the car.

Stacy watched him as he walked through the door and said a silent prayer that he would have the strength for what he was about to face.

The look on the face of the woman sitting behind the desk when Doug announced his name went from one of cheerfulness to one of deep sorrow. She was an older woman in her late fifties, with short hair and thick glasses. "Please have a seat, and I'll let the coroner know you're here."

Doug watched as she stood and walked down the hall, disappearing around the corner. He sat there, wondering how he would find the strength to get through this.

Hell, he had just returned from the war, and this was going to be harder than anything he had faced over there. He kept going over in his mind of all the different training he had received while in the corps, but nothing had prepared him for something like this.

Doug's heart broke once he realized the first time, he would see his little girl in person would be to claim her body and then put it in the ground. He would never know what it was like to hug her, to hear her laugh, or even cry. He would never know the joy of hearing the words, "Read me a story, play tea party with me, or most of all…I love you, daddy."

Then there was Donna, she had been the strength in his life. It was not fair that she had to face something like that alone.

Damn it, I should have been there to protect you, but I always knew you had a lot of fight in you, girl, he said silently with a smile on his lips.

I bet that sorry bastard never thought you would go after him the way you did. I'm so sorry I was not there for you when you needed me the most.

The sound of footsteps brought him out of his thoughts. "Sir, please follow me."

They walked with only the sound of their footsteps echoing off the walls of the hallway like empty promises of a life that should have been. As they made the turn at the end of the hall, Doug whispered, "I want to see my daughter first."

The sudden sound of his voice startled the woman making her stumble. "Of course, anything you want."

The nervous woman looked at Doug and wished that she knew something to say to make this easier on him; however, no words came to her.

Both of them continued walking to the end of the hallway, stopping in front of a set of double doors. Doug paused a moment, knowing these doors would take him to the painful vision that would live with him for the rest of his life.

The room was smaller than Doug had expected. When they entered the room, Doug saw a man whom he presumed was the coroner seated at a desk filling out some forms.

When the man noticed them come in the room, he stood and walked toward Doug, and introduced himself. "Good afternoon, my name is Dr. Petroff. I hope you don't mind, but I wanted to meet you and thank you for your service. I served in the Corps myself for ten years, and then I went and broke my ankle during training so I couldn't keep up anymore.

For this reason, I decided to go to medical school and serve my fellow man this way. I wanted to let you know if there is anything I can do to help, please, just ask." He was a pleasant man in his mid-sixties, and Doug was thankful for his kindness.

"Doctor, he wants to see his daughter first," the woman interrupted nervously.

She wanted to get back to her desk, as she never liked coming to this room when the families of the deceased were here to identify their loved ones.

"So, if I'm no longer needed..." she held her breath, as she looked at the doctor.

"Yes, that's fine. Thank you, Ms. Henderson," the doctor replied as he waved a dismissive hand at the door.

The woman did not waste a moment heading back out the door, "Thank you, Doctor."

The doctor turned and walked across the room where he stopped in front of a small door, he then reached for the handle and slowly pulled out the drawer.

The first thought to go through Doug's mind was how small the form was under the sheet. He noticed how his mouth went dry, and his heart seemed to stop beating in his chest.

How could his sweet, little daughter be lying there under that plain white cloth? How could she not be cold in there?

Hell, it's bone-chillingly cold in this room, he thought to himself as he looked down at the small figure lying there, wondering if he would ever again know the feeling of true warmth.

The doctor cleared his throat, bringing Doug out of his thoughts. He reached for the sheet and slowly pulled it back, revealing his daughter. Doug quickly closed his eyes, not wanting to see the image awaiting him. Realizing that he could no longer deny the nightmare before him, he braced himself and opened his eyes.

"She looks like an angel, sleeping peacefully." The words had escaped Doug's mouth before he realized what he had said.

The doctor looked down at the sweet, little one lying there, and said tenderly, "Yes, she does."

Doug had never known such pain in his life. There was his perfect little girl. He leaned forward and gently kissed her on the forehead, and then whispered, "Daddy loves you, baby.

I will always love you, and I know you are now in heaven with Mommy. I wish we could have had some time together. I had so many dreams, so many plans…" His tears dropped down onto her little face then ran down her cheek.

"Daddy's sorry that I wasn't here to protect you and Mommy from the evil man. Please forgive me," he cried as he reached down and gently wiped his tears from her face.

"Daddy needs to go and see Mommy now; I love you, Miranda Louise Mabry."

***

The sound of the drawer closing was the worst sound he had ever heard, that was until Dr. Petroff reached for the next small door and pulled out the drawer. The form lying under this sheet was larger, approximately five and a half feet long. Doug did not think he could feel any worse, but he was wrong. The sight of her beautiful face appearing from under the white sheet made his knees buckle beneath him, and the room began to spin. He did not realize that he was hanging onto the side of the drawer to keep from falling. It was only when the doctor reached out to help stabilize him that he became aware he felt dizzy as if he was in a fog.

The place where the bullet had entered the side of her head looked like Hollywood make-up for a horror movie, except there was no blood. He ran his finger along the incision marks on her hairline from the autopsy, noticing the small neat stitches. "You do good work, Doctor. Thanks for taking the extra time to make her look the best you could."

He leaned forward and kissed her gently on the lips, "I love you, Donna, you are my love, and I want to thank you for being my wife. I only wish we could have had more time together. I want you to know you did good, sweetheart. Miranda looks just like you and thank God for that," he smiled because he knew she would have said the same thing.

"Baby, Stacy said she has a beautiful headstone for you and Miranda, and I need to let her know what to put on it."

He looked at her as if she would open her eyes, but he knew he would never look into her beautiful eyes again.

"I don't know what to put on it, though; what does one say when their whole life lies beneath a piece of stone? How do I express how special you were in a few simple words?

How can a message let future generations fully understand how important you two were to me? Baby, I need your help; I don't know if I can do this without you."

Doug never knew a person could still be alive when their heart was dead; surely, this must be a medical first. He lifted himself back up, trying to wipe away the tears. Dr. Petroff understanding his embarrassment had acted as though he was looking through some forms on the counter next to them.

Doug turned toward the doctor and asked, "What do I need to do now?"

"There are some forms you will need to fill out, and Ms. Henderson will help you." The doctor reached down, grasped the sheet, and pulled it back over the beautiful face lying there, and then he closed the drawer.

"I can walk back up to the front with you if you'd like?" The doctor felt the pain radiating from Doug. How he hated this part of his job, there never were the proper words to say at this time.

"No, thank you; that won't be necessary. I'd rather be alone if you don't mind?" The last thing Doug wanted now was small talk. "Thank you for everything, Doctor."

Chapter 16

The Hunt for the Executioner

Doug hated cases like this. The only witness did not want to help, and the press was having a field day with it.

Angel of Death Decapitates Attacker or Angel of Death Swoops in To Save Woman from Certain Death!

He hated how they would glamorize such things just to make the story more interesting.

"Damn bloodsuckers!" Doug said to himself as he folded the paper and placed it on the corner of his desk.

He knew it was going to be next to impossible to solve this one since Miss Mathews was not willing to offer any more information about the man who had saved her.

To be honest, he did not blame her; just the thought of what that asshole had planned for her turned Doug's stomach. Doug also hated cases like this because they always brought back painful memories of Donna.

"Crap, I'm not getting anything done by sitting here; it's time to get to work."

He stood, gathered his notes, and reached for his coffee cup, but stopped at the sound of his telephone ringing.

"Shit!" He sat back down, then lifted the receiver up to his ear. "This is Detective Mabry. Another body found? Where? Okay, I'll head right out."

Doug could not believe the call; someone had found another murder victim. "What the hell is going on?"

He stood, grabbed his notes and coffee, and headed out the door to his car.

Doug was pleased the morning traffic had cleared. He was amazed at how people could spend so many hours of their day stuck in traffic while going to and from work, and somehow not go completely crazy. People would say that everything in Los Angeles was only twenty minutes away, but Doug knew that only depended on the traffic at the time.

Doug had often thought of moving to one of the outer suburbs, but the idea of driving every day in the bumper-to-bumper, stop and go traffic was unbearable.

Besides, his apartment was only a couple of blocks from the station on Wilcox, and his neighbors seemed to appreciate a cop living in the building. He would laugh whenever they would say, "You protect us from the bad people who don't understand girls like us."

He had often wondered what Donna would say about his neighbors. He lived in a small apartment building with six units, just off Santa Monica Boulevard in North Hollywood. At first, he was not sure about taking the apartment because the residents were a bit colorful, but once he saw the inside of the apartment, he decided to make it his home.

The building was three stories tall, with two units per floor, and he lived on the first floor. His neighbor was the owner of the building and an ex-burlesque dancer named Sally Silverlove. She was a sweet older lady who loved to share the tales of her 'performing' days in the old Burlesque shows.

She would sit for hours looking at an old photo album filled with pictures of a beautiful young woman with long legs and dark flowing hair, dressed in exotic costumes made of feathers and shimmering cloth. She had no family of her own, so Doug had adopted her as a surrogate mother.

His other neighbors were just as interesting. The occupants of the other four apartments were performers in a nightclub of female impersonators.

There was never a dull moment, but no one bothered Doug out of respect for his privacy.

As he pulled up to the crime scene and parked, a tall, young patrol officer walked up to his car and leaned into the open window.

"Are you Detective Mabry?" the young officer asked in a shaky voice.

Doug nodded, wondering why the officer seemed so upset.

"Sir, I'll take you to the body." He stepped back from the car and waited for Doug to join him.

They walked down the alley in complete silence, and Doug wondered why the young officer was acting so strange.

"You have secured this area, correct?" Doug asked to break the silence.

"Yes, Sir, we've made sure no one is anywhere near the victim, and that the media can't get close enough to take any pictures."

The young officer stopped about ten feet from a group of officers looking down at the body slumped against the wall.

"Sir, I need to get back out to the street, and make sure no one tries to get down here." He quickly turned around and headed back out of the alley before Doug had a chance to thank him.

"So, what do we have here?" Doug asked as he walked closer to the group.

A couple of men stepped aside, allowing Doug to get closer, and what he saw could him completely by surprise. In all of his days as a detective had he seen anything such as this. The body was leaning against the wall and sitting upright. He had his hands bound behind him, and his legs were duct-taped together at the ankles out in front of him.

Doug found himself looking into the eyes of this man; eyes froze wide with fear even in death. The sign placed on his lap gave a hint as to why he was chosen for this form of death, but to follow through with it had amazed Doug.

The sign had a simple message written on it, "Sodomite of the Innocent."

The scene seemed quite serene, as you would never have known the violent manner in which the man had died at first glance. His mouth was taped shut with the same duct tape used to bind him, and you could tell the perpetrator had taken the time to shave around the mouth, ensuring the tape stuck snugly to the skin.

A circle of blood had soaked through the groin area of his pants, and onto the ground, mixing with the dirt and trash.

Man, this is going to be a strange one, Doug thought to himself.

It took another twenty-five minutes to document the findings and for the coroner to arrive to make the pronouncement. There was nothing out of the ordinary until they removed the sign and saw that his unzipped pants showed a bloodied wound and his missing penis.

At the sight of this, two of the officers threw up on the ground, as the rest of them stood there in shocked disbelief. However, what sparked Doug's attention was when they turned the body over to examine his backside.

They found a slit was in his pants and the end of a metal rod protruding from it. "Oh, my God; what the hell is that?"

What happened to the man was something beyond imagination. The severed penis skewered onto a rod was rammed deep into the anus of the victim with such force that it nearly punctured through the skin of his abdomen. From all appearances, the victim did not die right away but instead had endured a slow and painful death.

Doug watched silently as the paramedics loaded the body on a stretcher to transport it to the Coroner's office, and he wondered what would drive someone to do this to another person.

"It shouldn't be too hard to figure the cause of death for this one." The officer standing next to Doug said with a nervous laugh.

"Man, what a horrible way to die!" He added, shaking his head from side to side.

"What...what did you say?" Doug had been deep in thought, so he did not hear the comment.

"Nothing, I was just thinking out loud, sorry, Sir." The officer suddenly realized that he should not have said what he did and wanted to distance himself from the whole thing.

Doug watched as the doors on the Coroner's van closed, and a sudden feeling of dread overcame him. "Damn!"

"Sir?" The officer questioned nervously. "I know I should have never said..."

Doug had no time for foolish conversation. "Be quiet, I wasn't talking to you; now get back to work!"

Doug did not like the feeling beginning to creep up inside of him. "Damn it! I know who did this: The Angel of Death," he whispered under his breath as he headed back to his car.

Chapter 17

On the drive back to the station, Doug kept replaying the scene in his mind.

To kill someone in such a gruesome manner showed genuine hatred for the victim.

"That's it! The clue must be in the sign left there on the victim's lap!" He said aloud.

First, there was the man who attacked Miss Lisa Mathews and got his head cut off because he was trying to rape and kill her. Now this man was violently murdered and had the sign saying, Sodomite of the Innocent placed on his lap.

Doug took a moment to go over the events again in his mind when it suddenly came to him.

"Can it be that simple, are these two killings linked? Are they the result of some vigilante who is killing those he believes do harm to the innocent?" Doug said to himself as he turned into the parking lot at the station.

He pulled into his parking space with a surge of excitement coursing through his body. He then headed inside to do some research on the computer.

It only took a few moments to pull up the rap sheet and pictures of the dead man in the alley. His name was Charles W. Fountene. He had served time for different drug-related charges, as well as petty theft. However, what caught Doug's attention was the section referring to this very same Charles as having been brought in for questioning in several cases of child rape.

All the victims were boys under the age of five, and each had been bound, blindfolded, and then brutally sodomized. Another interesting fact was he had worked for each of the victims' families, doing work as a handyman, giving him access to the boys.

The problem was the perpetrator of these crimes had been very careful not to leave any DNA evidence behind to identify him. The investigator in the cases believed he must have used latex gloves and a condom during the attacks and had made sure the victims never saw him. None of the children was able to identify Charles Fountene as their attacker, so he was released pending further developments in the case.

Doug was sickened to read how when they had released him from questioning, he had laughed and made the statement that they would never prove he had touched the little boys, and how the case against him would meet a dead end.

"It looks like the cases did meet an impasse and are now closed due to a little justice already administered to the sick bastard," Doug laughed quietly.

Doug understood the desire to act against a violation of the innocent, but to pronounce justice by acting as judge, jury, and executioner; both worried and excited him. He more than most understood the desire to see justice paid for heinous crimes.

Hell, there are too many times when a scumbag like him gets off because of some slick lawyer. Then they go out and repeat their crimes on more of the innocent.

Doug often had to do the same thing, but he was an officer of the law. It was his duty to bring the needed evidence to the courts so a judge and jury could pronounce the proper justice.

A smile crossed Doug's lips at the thought of that scumbag Charles W. Fountene, looking into the eyes of his executioner with the full knowledge of why he was about to die.

"I bet you never expected to die like that, did you?" Doug whispered to himself as he closed the browser on his computer.

A sudden thought hit him. "Do I really want to catch this vigilante executioner?"

He knew it was his job, but Doug also knew his heart would not be in it.

The rest of the day went by as usual. First, he looked in on the autopsy to see if there was any new evidence to help solve the mystery of the vigilante. Doug knew he might be reaching to tie the two cases together, but it made perfect sense with them committed in the same grotesque way.

The person who did this took pride in what they did and wanted his prey to know the same terror their victims had felt, but what kind of person would do something like that?

Was it just another sicko, wanting to get his jollies off by making sure his victims suffered?

If the decapitation was the only case involved, Doug might have thought it was the reason, but not after the one from today.

This one appeared planned and executed in a very precise manner, as he came prepared to deal out his deadly payment of justice. It took time to do everything; hell, he probably even lured the bastard there. Doug knew this case was going to be a hard one to solve because this person was smart, too smart to leave any tangible evidence behind.

The Coroner did not find anything that would give them any hope of proving who had killed Charles W. Fountene. Doug knew that he would have to get lucky to solve this one, and he hoped there would be no others before he could.

***

Doug looked at the clock on the wall across the room and realized it was late. He put the remaining paperwork in a folder and placed it in the basket on the corner of his desk.

"Well, there's nothing more I can do today," he quietly said to himself while he looked around the office, wondering what plans the others had for the evening.

Well, I guess it's time to go home, eat dinner, and catch some sleep.

He had often caught the look of excitement on the faces of his co-workers when they went home to their families for the day, but Doug would do the same lonely thing day after day. Sometimes a fleeting thought would float through his mind of how it would be to have a family to go home to again.

He closed his eyes, with the vision of Donna appearing in his mind. She was in her favorite blue dress with little flowers on the corners of a white-collar. She walked up to him, giving him a kiss and a hug, welcoming him home after a long day at work. He would hold her close, breathing in her fragrance.

God, she always smelled so good, he thought to himself.

After she had died, he tried spraying her perfume around the house to remind him of her, but it just was not the same. He could not bring himself to wash the bedding for weeks, attempting to hold on to her scent for as long as possible.

The sound of laughter from across the room brought Doug out of his daydream.

"Come on, those days are gone!" he said to himself with a mixture of anger and pain in his voice.

He always loved to go to that special place with Donna in his mind, but it was always so painful when he had to return to the real world.

"Ah, hell, time to go home," Doug muttered under his breath. He stood, took one final look at his desk to make sure things were in their proper place, and then headed for the door to the parking lot.

Chapter 18

When Doug parked his car in the parking area for the apartment tenants, he noticed Miss Sally standing in her doorway, waving for him to follow her inside. He was not in the mood for visiting after the long day, but he knew if he did not stop and see what she wanted, she would just come over to his apartment anyway.

He waved and smiled, letting her know he would be right there. *I love you, Miss Sally, but I'm not in the mood tonight,* he groaned to himself.

"Come on in, Dougie," she said with a shaky voice. He hated it when she called him that, but he knew that she thought of it as a term of endearment. He opened the screen door and stepped inside.

Her apartment was small like his; only with all of her things, it seemed much smaller. He walked to the overstuffed pink chair next to her and sat down. "What may I do for you today, Miss Sally?"

Her response surprised him, as the expression on her face was suddenly solemn.

"I know who killed those men on the TV news. He's done things like this before," she paused, then looked at Doug to respond.

"What do you mean he's done stuff like this before? I've never heard of a case like these around here before." Doug looked at her trying to figure out if she was in a clear state of mind, or just experiencing the effects of her advanced years. "Miss Sally, are you sure about this?"

"I'm quite sure, Dougie. You see, an old friend of mine from my performing days told me stories of someone who would kill people who had done terrible things and got away with it. This happened in Chicago around ten years ago. Three, no four people were murdered in about six-month span, and then nothing." She paused for a moment before continuing, "My friend said each one was killed in a similar way to what they had done to their victims. He would do horrible things to them; unbelievable things."

She stopped long enough to take a sip of her tea and clear her thoughts before she continued, "He never hurt anyone who hadn't hurt someone else. The police tried to figure out who he was, but he was too smart for them. Then the fact that no one on the streets wanted to help because they were thankful to him for punishing the bad people was another problem for the authorities.

One case that stuck out the most to my friend was what he did to a terrible man who had forced several young girls to perform oral sex on him. Then because of a high-priced, slick lawyer, he had gotten away with it. He was found dead in his house by his housekeeper, tied to his bed and completely naked," she paused a moment because the words were difficult to say. "He was lying there with his legs spread apart so you could clearly see his testicles were gone, and he had the words Child Rapist carved into his chest."

This time, she had to take a deep breath before continuing. "He also had a large dildo forced so far down his throat that he was unable to breathe, so he suffocated."

She looked at Doug with the strangest smile on her face. "I bet you're wondering what happened to his testicles? They found them during the autopsy in his stomach."

Doug sat dumbfounded, unable to speak. *Can it be true? Could this be the same person, or is this a copycat?* He looked at

Miss Sally and saw a worried look come across her face.

Her eyes met his, "Don't worry if this is the same person. You won't have anything to worry about because he only goes after the bad people."

Doug tried to muster a smile to calm her fears, but his mind was reeling.

This has happened before? The very thought of this terrified Doug, as it was now an entirely new ball game.

"Sweetie, I'm not worried about him being here because, in my books, he's on the good side. I'm just worried that you will have to choose," she frowned, now seeing the concerned look in his eyes.

"Choose, what do you mean? You're afraid I'll have to choose; choose what?" Doug was not sure if he liked the direction this conversation was going.

Miss Sally sat up in her chair, squared her shoulders, and spoke clearly and precisely. "You already know deep in your heart. Will you have the desire to stop him, or will you let him continue with his work?"

Doug did not know what to say because she was right. He was tired of bringing the scum of the earth in just to have some slick lawyer manipulate the jury into letting them back out on the streets to victimize again. However, it was his job to bring the vigilante in before he kills again.

Chapter 19

Doug had sat staring at the empty wall for so long that his dinner was now cold. No matter how hard he tried, he could not seem to shake Miss Sally's words from his mind. "You're going to have to choose."

He knew in his logical mind; there was no choice. The person had to be brought to justice for his crimes, but another idea kept creeping its way into his thoughts. Doug would never admit to it, but none-the-less it was there and boldly forcing itself to the forefront of his mind.

What would happen if he came face to face with this person? He knew in his heart that it was wrong to think these things, but if someone had taken care of the scum who had killed Donna and Miranda before that horrible day, then maybe…

"Knock it off! You can't be losing yourself in thoughts like that. You're an officer of the law, damn it!" he growled, as he swirled his fork around in the cold mashed potatoes and gravy.

No longer having an appetite, he walked to the trashcan, scraped the food off the plate, and put the plate and fork in the sink. "I'll wash the dishes later; I have some research to do," he groaned as he walked into the living room and sat at his computer desk.

While waiting for his computer to boot up, he wondered if this could be the same person.

Ten years is a long time to be doing this and never be caught, he thought to himself.

Maybe a little research on the Chicago cases will help shed some light on things.

If the same person had committed these crimes, Doug was going to find out quickly.

Miss Sally had told him about several newspaper articles on the rape cases. Apparently, the man was some sort of financial bigwig in Chicago, who had used his wealth and power to beat the rape charges. All the victims had come from poor families and easily frightened by the high-powered attorney for the defense during cross-examination.

Each of them had all easily identified the defendant in a lineup, but during questioning, they had caved and said they fabricated the charges in the attempt to extort money. With the help of his attorney and an excellent public relations person, the defendant was able to paint himself as the victim of greedy parents who had used their children for monetary gain.

To obtain access to the children, he had set up a charitable organization to help needy families get affordable housing after the loss of their homes from fire or financial hardship. He would then befriend the family by giving them clothing and other needed items. Then once he had the parents complete trust, he would invite their young daughters for a *fun day* where he would force them to perform oral sex on him. He had apparently gotten away with doing this for several years because he would threaten the girls into silence. He would tell them how he would hate for mommy or daddy to have an unfortunate accident, and then he would take out photos of a man shot in the head to drive home his point.

Then before he took them home, he would thank them for being such good little girls, give them some money, and tell them it was to help their family.

It had all worked out for him until the day he tried to lure twin sisters on a special outing with him, not knowing they were friends with one of his previous victims who had told them of what he did to her.

The parents of the twins had given him permission to take the girls to a party at the roller-skating rink, but when he arrived to pick them up, the girls had refused to go. They cried, saying that they did not want to go because of what had happened to their friend. He, of course, had denied everything and had acted hurt by the accusations, but the father of the twins called the police anyway.

The trial was a huge media event, with several children coming forward with accusations of the times he had taken them to the Special Place. Of course, none of them could ever tell the authorities where it was, only that it was dark and smelled funny.

Unfortunately, once his lawyers had finished with the children, the whole case had fallen completely apart. No matter what the children said, the defense attorney twisted their words into something entirely different from the truth.

It always had amazed Doug how an attorney could have someone on the stand say something one way, only to twist it into something else by distorting their words.

After lengthy questioning, the defense attorney had proven the allegations of forced sex were a lie by twisting the words of the children and their parents. He then went on to say, it was simply a plan to extort money from his client, thus destroying their claims of abuse.

The image created by the attorney for the defendant was a classic legal maneuver. He had spun a tale of the families conspiring to extort money from his client, and when he would not pay, they had called the police. He then went on about how the parents had freely sent their daughters with the defendant on numerous occasions so that clearly proved his client's innocence.

The side for the defense had person after person testifying on how he and the girls had been in public view at all times, just as he had testified. The owner of the pizza parlor testified how he had seen him several times with groups of children having pizza parties, and none of the children looked upset or scared. Next was the gate worker at the zoo, who had testified that she saw him on numerous occasions bring a group of children for a day of fun.

Person after person told of him doing good things for families and their children, but not once was there any mention of him being alone with a child.

When it was time for the parents to testify, the defense attorney swooped in like a bird of prey. He had asked the parents why they trusted this man enough to let him leave their house alone with their child.

"Do you think it was the wisest thing to do?" The defense attorney said with a grin.

Then the parent would respond by saying, "but he said there were other children in the limo, so I just thought…"

The lawyer then would cut them off by saying, "Ah, so there were other children there."

The parent at realizing this response was not good for their side, tried to correct their testimony. "I didn't see them, but why would he bring such a big car if it were only going to be for him and my child? I never thought he would…"

The lawyer would then move in close, saying in a low and accusatory tone, "Very true; why would he? So, your claims of him taking your child off to a private place to molest them are unfounded, are they not?

You did, however, enjoy the money he gave your family, but it was not enough for you, was it? You wanted more, didn't you?"

The lawyer continued his badgering form of cross-examination on parent after parent until the jury had no faith in the accusations. After a short deliberation, the jury acquitted him of all charges.

Doug closed the browser and sat motionlessly with his blood boiling in his veins.

"The bastard got what he deserved!" Doug knew in his heart it was wrong to take the law into your own hands, but sometimes...

He then read about the other three strange murders around the same time, and all of them had the same Modus operandi. Each one involved a vicious attack against the guiltiest of victims. One involved a home invasion/robbery where the attacker brutally beat an elderly woman, leaving her to die a horrible and painful death. The next was the rape and murder of a young college student while she was walking back to her apartment after an evening at the library. Then the third was a thirteen-year-old boy shot down in the street by a nineteen-year-old gang-banger wannabe, who only wanted to know what it would feel like to kill someone.

It had intrigued Doug how these people were chosen for *justice*. This person did not choose people randomly, he only went after those who had escaped paying for their crimes, and he always made sure that they knew the reason for their punishment.

He wanted them to experience what they had done to their victims; Doug sat up straight, his eyes wide with understanding.

"This guy made each person know the undeniable truth of justice," the words flowed from Doug's mouth with the sudden realization of what the murderer's motive was.

"So that's what this is all about? He makes them pay for their crimes by the shedding of their own blood; an eye for an eye: Pure Justice."

Chapter 20

The morning sun shone brightly through Doug's bedroom window, announcing a new day. Doug had spent the entire night looking for more unsolved cases matching those from Chicago, as well as those from the last few days. He was surprised to find there were small clusters of gruesome, unsolved murders, each involving someone who had escaped paying for their crimes scattered across the country over the last thirty-plus years.

Doug had marked each of the cities on a map where similar murders had taken place, and he began to notice a pattern. The vigilante started in Los Angeles and then moved to the next nearest one until finally ending in San Francisco and the murder of six anti-war protesters in the early 1970s.

Is that where it all started? Doug wondered as he stared at the map.

He decided to study the articles written about the case in San Francisco involving the group of anti-war protesters that had been found brutally tortured to death. The articles explained how they were acquitted of the gruesome murders of two soldiers who had recently returned from Vietnam.

The trial lasted several months, but with the ability of their attorney to cast doubt on the evidence and a sympathetic judge, it was no surprise when the jury granted them an acquittal.

The articles mentioned how the parents of the two slain soldiers had sat in the courtroom every day, watching as the entire case fell apart. Then on the day when the Judge had allowed crucial evidence stricken from the record, Mr. Smitten, the father of one of the slain soldiers, had stood screaming how the trial was nothing more than a joke. He then said how someday they would pay for the murder of his son.

He went on to say how everyone knew they were guilty, but that justice was not served because of a corrupt lawyer, and a self-serving judge who allowed his personal political beliefs to sway his court. The distraught man then pointed to the Judge and told him that the blood of his son was on his hands if he allowed his murderers to go free. Mr. Smitten then grabbed his chest and collapsed to the floor.

The day they found the murdered anti-war protesters, the media had gone wild with stories of revenge and retaliation. The police had tried to link both fathers of the slain soldiers to the murders but were unable. Mr. Childers had returned to Wyoming soon after the end of the trial, and Mr. Smitten was still in the hospital recovering from a heart attack.

The police had wondered if political reasons might also be the reason but were unable to find any further leads. It seemed that anyone who may have had a reason for revenge had already left the city.

Doug suddenly had an uneasy feeling come over him.

What about the third, returning soldier? He thought to himself. *One of the articles did refer to a friend who had returned with them from Vietnam.*

The report stated that the three had been friends while in Vietnam, but the third one had stayed behind at the hotel that morning. It continued to say how he was the one to identify the bodies and how shaken up he was by the whole thing. According to the records, he had left and returned home a few days later, so he was also cleared as a suspect. Then Doug found something, which piqued his interest.

A reporter had spoken to Mr. Smitten once they released him from the hospital, and he was more than willing to share his thoughts on the killings. He had said that while he was in the hospital recovering from his heart attack, an angel told him those who murdered his son would soon pay and that justice would be served. He went on to say that he was glad they had met their deaths in such a violent way, so they would know firsthand of the fear and pain his son had endured at their hands.

Angel? Where else had he heard that term used? He reached for the stack of local newspapers on the table; opened the last one on the pile, and there it was, Angel of Death Decapitates Attacker.

Can this be the same angel that Mr. Smitten said came to him while he was in the hospital? Doug wondered, as he folded the paper and returned it to the pile with the others.

Doug decided he would do some more research, the third soldier, and what happened to him.

***

"Thank you, Mr. Rathborn, I appreciate all the information. Your father must have been a kind man to have been so willing to help the Braxton family the way he did," Doug said as he hung up the telephone.

Doug had learned that Ted Braxton, the third returning soldier was from a small town in Southeast Texas.

After the acquittal, Ted gave his family property to Mr. Rathborn, Sr. and his wife to do with as they thought best and was never heard from again. Doug had run a check on his military record and found it was exemplary, as he had served with honor and distinction.

Doug learned that while Ted Braxton was in Vietnam, he had saved his unit from a sniper attack. While the sniper had the unit pinned down, picking them off one by one, Ted had snuck up behind the sniper, slit his throat, and saved the men from his unit from certain death.

However, the one thing that stood out as Doug continued reading was the name the men had given Ted while serving in Vietnam: The Executioner.

"This guy would have the knowledge and inner fortitude to do something like this,"

Doug said to himself as he started another pot of coffee.

The problem was that no one knew where he had been for over thirty years. His family was all dead, and no one from his hometown had heard any news of him since he had returned to San Francisco the last time. He had stayed at the same hotel and even had his room paid for by Mack Childers' father, but he checked out the same day as Mr. Childers and told the desk clerk he was returning home.

"But, where did you go, Ted?" Doug said aloud to himself.

"Did you begin traveling around this country and serving up justice in your own special way?" The very thought of this brought a chill of excitement to Doug.

Can this be the break needed to solve those two cases, as well as all the others? He knew this was the direction he needed to go, but where should he start?

How do you find someone who has been a ghost for over thirty years? Doug knew just the place to begin looking, and that was on the streets with those who lived a difficult lifestyle.

Chapter 21

It was noon when Doug pulled his car into the parking area at Prospect Park. He knew this was the place to come if you wanted to learn what was happening in the underbelly of the streets. He got out of his car and headed through the park to where the homeless had created a tent city.

As Doug got closer to where they were, he wondered what type of response he would get from the residents. He knew once they found out he was the law, they might just close down and refuse to answer any questions.

He saw a small group of men gathered under a tree and decided that would be the best place to start. When Doug approached the group, they turned and briefly looked at him, then went back to their conversation.

"Excuse me; I'd like to ask you a few questions," Doug said, as he reached the group.

"I'm Detective Mabry of the Los Angeles Police Department, and I'd like to know if any of you have information about who may be the vigilante that killed the two men recently?"

He waited for anyone to answer, but no one did. *Okay, so you want to play silent. That's fine; we'll just try another angle and see what you think of it,* he thought to himself.

"I know you all talk about what's going on out here on the streets. I also know that I'm the last person you want to speak with, but there's a problem with that line of thinking. You see, a man is killing people most gruesomely, so if you don't want to be next on his list, you might just want to help me with some information." Doug held his breath while he waited to see if this little nudge would get a better response.

"Ain't no one here gonna help you catch him," a man said while stepping out of one of the tents.

"He ain't gonna kill anyone who don't deserve it, so we ain't gonna help you stop him," the man smiled as he walked over to face Doug.

Doug estimated the man to be in his mid-sixties with long hair and a beard hanging to the middle of his chest. His clothes were tattered and dirty, and the soles of his shoes appeared to be made of duct tape.

"I know you're all probably scared of him, but I can assure you…" Doug did not get to finish his statement before he was interrupted.

"We ain't scared of him. Hell, we're all glad he's here. He's gettin' rid of a few scumbags you law boys don't seem to be able to catch. You might as well look somewhere else for help, cause you ain't gonna get any here," the old man chuckled as he reached up to swat a fly away from his face.

This response surprised Doug. He had never expected the people on the streets would want to protect him.

"You know that you're breaking the law if you're harboring him, do you understand? I'm sure that none of you wants to find yourselves in legal trouble by withholding evidence." Doug prayed this would get someone to begin talking.

"Mister, you can cuff me now if you want to, but I ain't sayin' nothin' to help you find him. If he's gettin' them off the streets, then he's a good and decent man in my eyes. I might not be a fine and upstandin' person like you, but I know when someone is doin' somethin' good. Since he's taken care of those two, we all sleep better at night."

The old man looked at the others gathered around who were now nodding in agreement. "And all the bad guys on the street are finally feelin' scared."

Doug stood there, not sure of what to say. The old man was right about one thing; the streets were safer without those two around.

"I understand what you're saying, and I totally agree, but you must understand that we can't have someone going around taking the law into his own hands. That's what the police and courts are for."

The old man laughed, "The police and the courts, you gotta be jokin'! Officer, you have to admit it must frustrate the hell out of you to catch someone, only to have some slick lawyer and the judge turn him back out on the streets. Well, we folks who live here don't much like it either. They love to rob us of what little we may have or hurt us just for shits and grins. Hell, our lives may not mean much to most folks, but we'd like to be able to live without puttin' up with all that crap." The rest of the group chimed in their agreement.

"Hell, ole Chuck over there was robbed and beaten plum near to death a few weeks ago by a guy who had been in and out of jail several times for attackin' people. He did it because he was angry that Chuck only had two dollars on him at the time."

The old man paused, then looked Doug directly in the eyes before continuing, "We're tired of bein' afraid, and if this man wants to get rid of some of those bad men, then we welcome it."

Realizing that he was not going to get anywhere with these people, Doug reached into his pocket, took out a business card with his telephone number on it, and handed it to the old man.

"Here, take this, and if you change your mind, please call me, alright?"

The old man held up the card closer to his eyes, carefully looking at it, "Detective Mabry, is that your name, hmm? Well, Detective, don't expect any calls from us, but I'll keep your card just in case."

As he placed the card into his jacket pocket, he looked back up into Doug's eyes and said, "You seem like a nice enough law officer, but can you tell me one thing? Do you really want to catch this guy, or are you just goin' through the motions?" He smiled, waiting for the reply.

The words hit Doug like a sledgehammer. Earlier, while sitting at home, that very thought had crossed his mind, but to hear the words spoken by someone else drove the point home. Did he really want to catch him, or was he just going through the motions of pretending to find him?

All those doubts swirled through Doug's mind, and before he could respond to the question, the old man laughed again and said, "Yeah, I thought so. You don't want to arrest him, cause you think what he's doin' is the right thing too."

Doug looked at the old man, not sure of what to do or say. *Was that the truth? Am I only going through the motions to make myself feel better about the fact that I secretly like what he is doing?*

"Sir, that's not what's happening here. I'm only trying to stop a vigilante from killing more people. We, as a society cannot have someone going around and taking the law into their own hands. We are a country of laws and..." but he was cut off before he could finish.

"Laws are easily bent by people who want to do so for the greater good. Hell, they are bent every day by those wantin' to gain power and money. You can't stand there and tell me there ain't been a time in your life that you would have loved to have done what he's doin'." The old man smiled as he looked deeply into Doug's eyes.

Doug knew he was right; he had felt that way after Donna and Miranda were murdered. The man who shot them was given a sweet deal from the prosecutor because he wanted a conviction. The worst thing was when the Prosecutor told Doug that it would be the best way to ensure he paid for his crimes. He was only given twenty years with the chance of early parole for good behavior, so what kind of justice was that?

On the day he was sentenced, Doug decided to go into law enforcement. He did so with the hope of cleansing some of the anger from his soul by taking people like the man who had destroyed his family off the streets. He hated the idea of anyone experiencing his pain, so he had made it his life's mission to arrest those who would do harm to others.

Doug looked at the old man, unable to respond.

"Yep, I thought so. Detective, we appreciate you takin' the time out of your day, but you're just wastin' your time here. I got your phone number in case anything changes." With that last statement, the old man turned and went back to his makeshift tent and disappeared inside.

***

Doug walked back to his car, not at all pleased with the outcome of his visit. He did have to admit to himself that the old man was right about one thing, he really did not have a burning desire to arrest this man. He knew it was wrong, but he just could not help the way he felt.

For years, he had watched, as violent offenders would get away with some of the most horrific crimes because a slick lawyer twisted the evidence. How many times had he fantasized about doing some of the very same things as this vigilante?

Come on, I know better than to think this way, he chided himself.

I need to keep myself on the correct path, and find him before he kills the next person! Doug started his car and headed back home to his empty apartment.

"Good afternoon, Dougie." The shaky voice of Miss Sally came from behind the screen door. "Would you like to come in for a bit, and have a nice glass of iced tea with me?"

"No, thank you, I have something important I need to do. Maybe some other time, okay?" he smiled as he unlocked the door to his apartment.

"Okay, then I'll see you later." The disappointment was evident in her voice.

Miss Sally cared deeply for Doug and would always look forward to his visits.

He quickly opened his door and slipped inside before she could say anything else. As he closed the door behind him and walked to the kitchen, his cell phone began to ring. He pulled it out of his pocket and answered, "Hello."

The voice on the other end was soft-spoken, "Is this Detective Doug Mabry?"

"Yes, it is," Doug replied.

"I heard you were looking for me. I thought I would contact you so that we could have a little talk about things," the man said in a calm and reassuring voice.

"Looking for you? Are you who I think you are? Are you the vigilante who murdered the two men recently?"

Doug tried to remain calm, but he wondered if the caller could hear his heart pounding in his chest.

"Well, it all depends on how you look at things. Some people may call it murder, while others think of it as dispensing justice," he chuckled.

Doug pulled himself together and continued, "In the eyes of the law, what you are doing is considered murder. You just cannot go around killing people in the name of justice."

The phone was silent for a moment before the man responded, but this time, he spoke in a much firmer voice. "I used to trust the system. I had always believed that justice would prevail, but the system proved my faith wrong. I lost someone very dear to me, only to have that same justice system slap their families and me in the face by letting those guilty of destroying two precious lives to go free. I decided that day to make sure it would never happen again. I made it my mission to ensure that justice is paid in full to the victims of those crimes and..."

Doug interrupted, "but what about the two men you killed here? They hadn't killed anyone; why did you kill them?"

"That's true, Detective. They hadn't killed anybody; yet. I think of them like you would a rabid dog. It may not have bitten you yet, but why take the chance. Besides, the first one was trying to kill that young woman and would have if I had not stepped in and stopped him. I had seen him around the area, and I knew what kind of man he was. Hell, only a couple of weeks ago, he had beaten a homeless man because he didn't have enough money on him. For this reason, when I saw him attacking the woman, I decided it was time to remove him before he was able to kill her. The poor thing was so scared and weak after what she had gone through that she fainted into my arms."

He took a deep breath before continuing, "Now the one you just found, he was an entirely different story. I'm sure you learned all about him once you discovered who he was. He was doing terrible things to the most innocent, and for that, he had to be put down before he could do harm again. I decided to do it in a way that would send a message to any others who might consider doing what he had done. I watched him for several days, and I can tell you he had full intentions of doing his sick acts on more innocent children very soon. So, Detective, it's just like I said; it was like putting down a rabid dog."

Doug did not know what to say. He knew what this person was doing was wrong, but a part of him wanted to pat him on the back and thank him at the same time.

Doug took a deep breath, trying to choose his words carefully before he spoke. "Why are you calling me? You know it's my job to arrest you; is that what you're wanting? Are you calling to surrender?"

The response to his question surprised Doug. "Surrender? Hell no! I have no intention of surrendering. I just wanted to call and let you know why I'm doing what I do. I want you to know that I'm not some crazed nut who is going around killing people just to get his rocks off. I have never hurt anyone who did not deserve it. I do, however, have a question for you before we finish, Detective."

Doug was not sure if he wanted to know what the question was, but he went ahead and asked. "Okay, what do you want to know?"

"Do you honestly want me to stop?" He said calmly and then hung up the telephone.

Doug sat in stunned silence for a moment before realizing the dial tone buzzing in his ear, "Damn, he's gone!"

He immediately dialed the number on his caller ID, but it repeatedly rang without an answer.

"Crap! I need to learn more about this phone number!" Doug grabbed his keys and rushed out to his car.

Chapter 22

Doug was glad that it was a short drive to the department. As he turned into the parking lot, he prayed that he could trace the phone number and find the man before he committed any more murders.

The question, "but do you really want me to stop?" kept swirling around in Doug's mind.

Do I? Do I really want to stop him from doing what I have fantasized about doing so many times to the man who killed Donna and Miranda?

Doug knew his thoughts were wrong, but he could not help the way he truly felt.

Rage had burned inside of him the day he learned the man who had destroyed his life had only received a light sentence for the sake of assuring a conviction. He hated how politics always seemed to find its way into enforcing the law and pronouncing a punishment.

"Damn, I need to remember that I'm sworn to uphold the law, not administer justice!" he angrily said to himself as he parked his car.

He had turned off the ignition and was about to pull out the key when a little voice in the back of his mind chimed in. *You know what he's doing is against the law, but in many cases, it's the only way to stop some people.*

Doug slammed his hand on the steering wheel in frustration, "Damn it, I need to quit thinking this way! I know what has to be done; now, just do it!"

He reached for the door handle and pulled it with such force that he nearly pulled it off the door.

"Calm down before you break something, you damn fool!" he laughed to himself as he got out of the car.

***

It always amazed Doug how things never seemed to calm down at the department. While walking to his office, he looked around to see who was on duty and what was going on, marveling at how it always had the appearance of organized chaos.

"Hey, what are you doing here today? I thought you were off for the weekend," Officer Rick McCay asked while escorting a prisoner to the holding room.

"I am, but I needed to check on something," Doug responded, but not wanting to elaborate, he merely continued walking toward his office.

"Damn, you sure are dedicated! I would rather be out on a nice ride today. I bought a new Harley Davidson Fat Boy this week, and I'm itching to take her out on a road trip." Rick grinned, but once he realized Doug was no longer around, he returned his focus to the prisoner.

"I guess you won't be taking any rides for a while, will you?" He laughed as they disappeared down the hall.

***

Doug was glad to get to his office. He quickly sat at his desk and powered up the computer. As the computer booted up, Doug mulled over the phone conversation with the man. Doug did have to admit one thing; the man only killed those deserving.

Once the computer had finished booting up, he entered the link to look up the telephone number.   As he flipped his phone open and found the number, he wondered how the man had gotten his telephone number.

"The business card I gave the homeless guy; that's how he was able to get my phone number!" The words escaped his mouth with the sudden realization that maybe he had been there the whole time, listening to every word said.

As he typed in the number, Doug wondered again if he could have done the same thing in his grief for his loss.

"Damn, it's one of those disposable phones," he moaned, with disappointment in his voice.

He knew it was impossible to find the man this way, so he would have to figure out something else. He turned the computer off and decided to go back home to relax the rest of the weekend, but he knew it was only an empty plan on his part.

***

Doug pulled into the driveway of his apartment building and parked. He could not believe how he had become involved in the recent turn of events. He also wondered if his personal feelings would impede his investigation. While getting out of his car, he noticed two of the other tenants were sitting outside and enjoying the evening air.

Doug had to laugh to himself at their appearance as they were dressed in the most flamboyant outfits he had ever seen.

Sugar, as he liked to be called, was in a bright, pink swimsuit with a floral print wrap, and a pair of stiletto-heeled shoes that must have been a size eleven or twelve. Sitting next to him was Juliet, dressed in a strapless summer dress and wearing a big, floppy hat that nearly covered his face. Both of them were in full makeup and had brightly painted fingernails.

"Good evening, Detective," they both cooed, as he walked up the sidewalk.

"Good evening, ladies. I see you're enjoying the beautiful day. Be careful not to get too much sun, you wouldn't want to burn," Doug grinned, as he walked past them.

"We'll be careful. Thank you," Sugar giggled as he watched Doug disappear into his apartment.

He then turned to Juliet and said, "That is one fine piece of man. Too bad he doesn't go for us more exotic girls." With that statement, they both laughed and returned to their previous conversation.

***

Doug closed the door and then walked to the table where he had left the map with all the cities with the other murders clearly marked.

He looked at the map again. "It has to be you. It has to be the third soldier, Ted Braxton. Why the hell didn't I ask you when I had you on the phone?" he groaned. He decided to get some rest, so he gathered up the map and put it back in the drawer at the end of the counter.

Doug did not like how all of this made him feel. He had worked hard to bury the rage he felt at the lack of justice for the murder of his family, but with the recent events, it was bubbling to the surface again. He knew he should let it go, but he could not because it would creep into his dreams every night.

All those years ago, and it was still as painful now as it was then. Not even going to the academy, getting hired on with the police department, and then eventually working his way up to Detective had helped to purge the raw feelings of rage he held deep inside of him.

"I need to stop doing this; I'm only going to make myself crazy!" he groaned to himself as he walked to the refrigerator and pulled a frozen dinner from the freezer.

"I can't let this guy get under my skin. I just need to do my job and move on!"

Once Doug had finished his dinner, he straightened up the kitchen, and then he decided to relax and watch some television. However, he could not find anything of interest to watch, so he decided to clean his gun and try to clear his mind.

The coolness of the steel in his hands was like the touch of a trusted friend, and he found the time he spent cleaning the handgun to have a calming and soothing effect on him. Once he finished, he put it back into his gun belt and got ready for bed. As he drifted off to sleep, a new dream invaded his mind. This one was of a man walking toward him out of the shadows.

Chapter 23

The sound of someone pounding on the front door brought Doug out of his fitful sleep. "What the hell?" he groaned, reaching for his gun.

He sat up and looked at the alarm clock sitting on the bedside table. "Crap, it's only 3:25 in the morning! Who the hell could that be?"

Doug got out of bed, slipped on a pair of jeans and shoes, and walked to the front door. "Hold on, I'm coming…shit, you'll wake up the whole building!" He reached the door, looked out the peephole, and saw a frantic Juliet standing there.

"What the hell…" he said as he opened the door.

"Oh, thank God you're here. It's Sugar, she's…" the emotions were more than Juliet could handle.

"She's what? What's wrong with Sugar?" Doug grabbed Juliet by the arms, forcing him to calm down.

Juliet looked at Doug with mascara-stained tears streaming down his cheeks, then he answered in a quivering voice, "She's dead! He stabbed her, and now she's dead!"

The words slammed into Doug's mind with such force that he wondered if he had heard them correctly. "She's dead? Where is she, and have you notified the police yet?"

"No, I came straight to you. She's only half a block from here. We were visiting Suzette, two buildings down, and were walking home. Doug, he came out of nowhere and demanded our money! We told him that we didn't have any with us, but he grabbed Sugar's purse. Damn, she loved that damn purse and didn't want to give it up, so she fought back, and that's when he stabbed her. I knew I was next, so I ran here to get you." Juliet stood there looking at Doug with a fear-filled expression on his face.

"Crap, we need to call in and report this!" Doug quickly grabbed his cell phone and dialed 911. He told the operator there had been a stabbing and gave them the address, and then he informed them who he was and that he would be on the scene once they arrived. He quickly grabbed a jacket, his gun belt, and his badge, and then pushed Juliet out of the way so he could close the door. "Come on, show me where she is!"

***

Doug felt his heart skip a beat when he saw Sugar lying on the sidewalk. He knelt down by the body, and then suddenly heard a soft whimper.

"She's still alive!" he said excitedly, as the sirens grew louder from the approaching vehicles.

"Oh, my God, Sugar…please, don't leave me!" Juliet cried out, reaching for Sugar.

"Stay back!" Doug shouted as a patrol car pulled up to the curb next to them, followed by an ambulance.

"The victim is still alive!" Doug yelled, reaching down to apply pressure to the wound.

"Step back, we have it!" One of the paramedics shouted; as they rushed up to Sugar and then knelt down to begin working on him.

Doug stood and moved back next to Juliet. As he looked down at the limp and bloodied figure lying there, he wondered if Sugar would pull through. He had to admit that despite their strange lifestyle, he liked having Sugar and Juliet as neighbors.

"I don't understand, why would he do that to her? She told him that she didn't have any money, but he called her a liar, and then he just stabbed her," Juliet sobbed, overcome with grief at the sight of all the blood.

"Please, you have to save her," he pleaded.

The paramedics did not respond, but lifted Sugar and placed him on the gurney, and then pushed it into the ambulance.

"Please take me too. I don't want to leave her!" Juliet cried while trying to get into the back door of the ambulance.

The patrol officer grabbed Juliet and pulled him away from the doors. "Stay back, you need to calm down, or I'll have to cuff you!"

"I'm sorry, but you can't go along. Now get back so we can leave!" the paramedic said before he closed the doors.

"No, don't leave me here! I need to be with her!" Juliet cried while flailing about like a fish on the riverbank. "Let me go, I need to be with her!"

Realizing things were about to get out of control, Doug cupped Juliet's face in his hands, looked him directly in the eyes, and firmly said, "You need to calm down. I'll take you to the hospital to be with Sugar, but first, you need to stop all this foolishness and behave yourself. Do you understand?"

"Okay, I promise," he said with his body going limp against the firm grasp of Doug's hands.

"Officer, I'm going to take Miss Juliet to the hospital, and then I'll go to the station and make a statement. I know she needs to give a report of what happened here, but she is in no condition to do it now." Doug knew there was nothing more for him to do with the rest of the officers marking off the area for the investigation.

"Come on, Juliet, let's get you to the hospital," Doug said in a reassuring voice.

The officer then released Juliet and turned to face the rest of the gathering group.

***

It had proved to be a long night for Doug. Once he had taken Juliet to the hospital, he then gave his statement at the station. It was well into Sunday morning before he finally returned home.

"I'm so tired of all this crap!" he moaned to himself as he walked into the kitchen to start a pot of coffee. He knew he should get some sleep, but he also knew if he did, he would never sleep that night, and he had to go back to work the next morning.

As he waited for the coffee to perk, he decided to relax in his recliner.

***

The room was dark with a strange, glowing mist swirling in the center. Doug tried to see a way out of the room, but there appeared to be no escape. He turned again toward the mist and watched as it transformed into a familiar shape, "Donna!"

"What are you doing to stop this, sweetheart?" The words seemed to come from inside of the mist.

"What do you mean? I'm a police detective; I'm working hard every day to protect people from harm," he moaned, the frustration clear in his voice.

"I know you are doing your best, but what are YOU doing to stop this?" The question was asked again.

"I don't understand what you mean...what more can I do?" The pain in his voice was now tangible.

"Search your heart for the answer, and you will find it there." The glow from the mist now grew faint, "I love you, and I'm always with you." With those final words, the mist was gone, and Doug was alone in the darkness.

"No, wait, please don't leave me!" he pleaded as he stepped forward trying to find Donna in the darkness. "Please don't leave me!"

Ring…ring…ring… The sound of his cell phone brought Doug out of the dream. "What the hell?" he groaned, fighting to regain his senses. "Hello?"

"I just wanted to let you know that I have taken care of the man who stabbed your neighbor," he said in a calm voice.

"Oh, God, please don't tell me you killed him!" The thought of another gruesome murder was more than Doug could handle at that moment.

"No, I didn't kill him, but I did make an example of him. He will never hurt anyone again. You see, it's difficult to rob and stab someone with no hands." He laughed at the memory of the man begging for mercy, and the look of fear on his face when he learned of his fate.

"You did what? You cut off his hands?" Doug could not believe what he had just heard.

This guy is crazy! "You can't go around doing these things; you need to leave it to the police!"

"I thought you would be pleased that I didn't kill him. This will send a message to any others who may be thinking of doing the same thing. He didn't care about your neighbor, did he? I hear that Sugar is going to make it, which is good. You know for yourself that it could have gone the other way," he waited for a response.

Doug knew he was right. Sugar could have died from that wound and would have ended up being just another senseless murder victim.

"You're right, but it still doesn't justify what you did."

"Maybe, maybe not, but the city now has one less scumbag to worry about. You know, you still haven't asked me the question," he said, with his voice now growing soft.

This statement caught Doug off guard. "Asked you what question?

"If I'm who you think I am. I'm sure you've put it all together by now, am I correct?" He said with a serious tone in his voice.

Doug could not believe this strange turn in the conversation. "Yes, I have. You started all this when your two friends were murdered in San Francisco after you all returned from Vietnam. You're Ted Braxton, aren't you?" Doug held his breath and waited.

"Yes, I am." The feeling of finally hearing the words brought a sense of release that surprised Ted. He had not used his name for thirty-four years, and it felt good to hear someone say it again.

"But why would you do this? You're a decorated war hero, a Marine! Whatever happened to Duty and Honor?" Doug hated the way this made him feel.

Doug could not stand the idea that Ted was a brother in arms and had chosen to take the law into his own hands.

While researching Ted Braxton's military background, he was surprised to learn how Ted had saved his unit from a sniper, as well as several other heroic actions he had done while serving in Vietnam. To know that he had turned into nothing more than a vigilante was heartbreaking for Doug.

"Don't you ever question my feelings of Duty and Honor! I did my duty only to return home and find a country that hated everything I stood for and believed. They murdered my friends in the name of peace and destroyed the promise of lives not yet fulfilled. I made a promise to a mourning father that I would see justice was paid for the murder of his son, and I always keep my promises." He said this with a mixture of both anger and pain in his voice.

Doug did not know what to say. He understood the rage of having someone you cared for taken from you in such a manner, but to respond in the way that Ted had was beyond comprehension. "You know I have to stop you, don't you?"

"Yes, I understand that you must do your duty, but before we get to that stage of our relationship, I have a request."

"A request, what do you want?"

"I need time to finish what I've started. I'm not asking for much, just a few more days, and then I'll let you do your duty," Ted said with a hint of sadness in his voice.

"I don't understand what you're asking. What have you started? Please don't tell me someone else is going to die."

What can he possibly be up to now? Doug thought to himself.

"All will be revealed in its proper time. I look forward to the day when we can sit and talk, Doug. Please don't think too badly of me. I'm not a monster. I'm only someone trying to make a difference with what he knows how to do best. I'm The Executioner, I kill, and I'm damn good at it." With those words, he hung up the telephone.

"Damn it, what are you up to, Ted?" Doug had a sinking feeling that he was not going to like what Ted had planned.

"Oh well, there's nothing I can do now," he groaned as he walked to the kitchen to get a cup of coffee and something to eat.

Doug knew it was late, so he decided to surf the internet for a while. "Damn it, why did I have to find out it was you, and why can't I bring myself to report what I've learned?"

He hated to know the person who had committed all those horrible crimes was someone like Ted Braxton. Everything he had learned about Ted was that he had always been a good and law-abiding citizen. He had enlisted straight out of high school and served honorably in Vietnam, but all that apparently changed when he got back to the states.

Doug had never faced the sort of rejection from the American people as those who served during the Vietnam War, and for that, he was most thankful. He could not imagine how one would feel to have people screaming things such as "Baby Killer" at you when you walked by them.

As the evening grew late, Doug felt himself drifting off to sleep.

"Damn, I better go to bed." He hated to sleep because the memory of the day Donna and Miranda died always visited him in his dreams.

Chapter 24

The sound of the alarm brought Doug out of his deep sleep. "What the hell?" He sat up, trying to get his bearings and suddenly realized something was different. He felt rested, in fact, more rested than he had in years. However, what surprised him the most was that he had slept the entire night with no memory of any terror-filled dreams.

For the first time since Donna and Miranda were murdered, Doug realized that he had a dreamless night. As he climbed out of his bed and walked to the bathroom to take a shower, he wondered what had brought about this long-awaited surprise.

Doug closed his eyes with the warm and invigorating water flowing over his body. He marveled at how alive he felt for the first time in years, as though someone lifted a terrible weight from his shoulders.

Then the thought came to him...*Ted Braxton!* Ted had shown him the way he could begin to purge his pain, and not by copying what he did, but by learning from it.

Ted had said never to question his honor because he only killed the guilty. Doug knew Ted's way of thinking was wrong, but he also understood why he felt the way he did.

For too long, the guilty escaped paying for their crimes because of shoddy police work, lawyers twisting the facts, and judges not following the rule of law. Doug had seen it himself far too often over the years. For this reason, for someone like Ted to come along and dispense justice himself was entirely understandable.

While Doug sat at his table drinking a cup of coffee and eating some toast, he wondered where this would all lead. He knew he would have to stop Ted from killing again, but he did not know how, or if he even wanted to.

It would be so easy to turn a blind eye, but to do so would go against everything Doug had always believed.

What was it that Ted had said? I only need a few more days. What did he mean by that?

Doug took another sip of coffee then looked at his watch, "Damn, I better get to work!" As he walked out the front door, he was curious about what the new day would bring.

"Good morning, Dougie. Are you off to work?" Miss Sally said through her front screen door.

"Good morning. Yes, but I need to get going, or I'll be late," Doug said, as he locked his door and turned to go to his car.

"I talked with Juliet this morning, and she said it looks as though Sugar will recover. They said she should get to come home soon."

Sally had always liked Sugar and Juliet. They were wonderful tenants who paid their rent on time and never gave her any problems. She always loved when they would come to visit. They would share beauty secrets with each other and talk about performing.

"Doug, may we talk for a moment, please?" She held her breath while waiting for his response.

The seriousness in her voice made Doug stop and turn to look at her. He knew he was going to be late, but he also sensed what she had to say was important and could not wait.

"Okay, but only for a few minutes." He reached for the screen door handle, and then opened the door, stepping inside. "What's going on?"

Sally did not know where to begin. She looked at him, wondering how he would take the information. However, she also knew it was time for him to know the complete truth.

For many years, she had held the secret close to her heart out of respect and gratitude, but *he* had told her it was time to share their secret. "Doug, I have an envelope for you. It's from a mutual friend, and he feels it's time to give this to someone who would understand."

She reached over to her end table, picked up a large yellow envelope, and held it up for Doug to see.

The severe tone of her voice surprised Doug, and he was surprised at how she had not called him Dougie as she normally did. Doug took the envelope from her, noticing the weight of its contents. He looked at Sally with a questioning look, but also found himself unable to speak.

"Yes, Doug, I see the questions in your eyes. Please, sit down at the table and open it. All your questions will be answered by its contents." These words were said with such tenderness that Doug feared what he would find.

He walked to her desk in the corner of the room and set the envelope on the desktop. He sat in the chair, unsure if he wanted to see its hidden contents.

What was it that she said? All of my questions will be answered from its contents, but what questions did she mean?

The words swirled wildly in Doug's mind as he stared down at the worn envelope with nothing identifying it or its mysterious contents. Realizing that he had no choice, Doug drew in a deep breath and opened the envelope.

***

"Why didn't you tell me you knew who he was?" Doug was surprised to see the letter requesting that he handle the necessary final arrangements after Ted's death. The enclosed letter went on to state how Ted believed that Doug would affirm his legacy as a man who had served his country with honor. Doug then found the paperwork for a burial plot in Texas, with a note explaining his desire to be buried next to his parents and brother.

Sally quietly sat while Doug read the letter and looked over the contents of the envelope, waiting for the questions she knew would come.

Doug finished looking through the paperwork, and then looked up at Sally with his mind spinning and full of questions.

"You want to know why I have this, don't you?" she asked with a smile on her lips.

"Well, it's a hell of a long story, so let me see where to begin." She closed her eyes and allowed the memories of that day nearly twenty years ago when she first met the mysterious hero, flow into her mind.

***

"It had been eighteen years since I had retired when I decided to go to a reunion for Burlesque dancers in New Orleans. I had gone several times during my dancing career and had always loved the city with its exciting culture. If I hadn't bought my little apartment building here in West Hollywood, I more than likely would have retired in New Orleans," she paused a moment, gathering her thoughts before continuing.

"One evening after dinner, while walking back to my hotel with another retired dancer, Kimberly Champagne, a pair of young men stopped us and demanded our purses. I knew better than to provoke them and held out my purse, but Kimberly panicked and began screaming for help. This, of course, caused the young man across from her to react by grabbing her and stabbing her in her throat. He then looked her in the eyes and growled, *Shut up bitch*, while he grabbed her purse."

Sally wiped the tears from her eyes as the emotions of that horrible night came flooding back to her.

"The one that held a knife on me after seeing what had just happened realized that things were out of control. He grabbed my purse then yelled, 'Damn it; we weren't supposed to hurt them!' I couldn't believe what had just happened. I just stood there, shaking with fear until I heard a strange noise and turned to see the blood spraying from between Kimberly's fingers as she tried to stop the bleeding. I could see the look of terror on her face, as her color faded away to be replaced with a look of cold death on her once beautiful face." The tears streamed down Sally's face as she thought back to that horrible night, but she pushed onward.

"I reached for her, as she crumbled to the ground, and then I screamed for help. There was nothing I could do. I just sat there helpless and watched as Kimberly died in my arms. Then the police arrived moments after her last gasp of life. They asked me the usual questions, but they said the chances of catching the bastards who killed her and had stolen our purses were slim."

The painful memory of that day ripped at Sally's heart. "I didn't care about my damn purse! Everything in it was replaceable. I only wanted justice for Kimberly. She didn't deserve to die for the few dollars in her purse! She was only scared, and he didn't need to do that to her!"

Sally wiped the tears from her eyes before continuing, "Kimberly's funeral was an interesting experience, to say the least. Of course, all of her family members were there, as well as half of the town. She was from a very nice family from Shreveport, Louisiana. None of them had understood her desire to be an exotic dancer, but they loved and supported her the best way they knew how. I have to say that the service was beautiful. Everyone shared stories of their friendship, and the love they had for her. I will never forget the outpouring of affection that day. To have people from such different lives come together to share their memories of one special lady was truly moving." Sally looked into Doug's eyes, seeing a look of acknowledgment in them.

Sally drew in a deep breath and exhaled slowly. "I came home the day after Kimberly's funeral, and I never left again. I felt safe here, so I decided to leave my Burlesque days behind me and focus on my new life and my little apartment building here in West Hollywood. A few weeks later, I received a surprising letter from Kimberly's sister in Shreveport. In the letter, she said how one day she had found Kimberly's purse sitting on her front porch with a note saying, *Justice paid in full*. Her sister had told her that everything appeared to be in the purse. Even the cash was there, but she had no idea who had returned it, or what the note meant. Her husband decided to contact the New Orleans police department to alert them, thinking it could be crucial to the investigation; however, what he learned surprised and pleased the entire family. The officer on the case was not at all surprised to receive the call from Kimberly's brother-in-law. He informed him that they were closing the investigation into Kimberly's murder because the case had been solved. The officer said they had found the body of a man in the same neighborhood where Kimberly was murdered with his neck cut and a note attached to his body saying, Justice-Paid in Full. The knife was still in the man's throat, and the only fingerprints on it were his own. The officer went on to say what surprised them the most was just a few feet away from the body; they had found a bound and gagged man with all of his fingers cut off. The man was overcome with fear and pain. He was half-crazed and kept repeating the same words, Thou shalt not steal. The terrified man confessed to how they were responsible for Kimberly's death, and that they had to pay for their transgression with An Eye for an Eye."

Sally sat with her eyes closed, completely at peace. "They deserved everything they got, and I prayed someday to thank the wonderful person who had made those two assholes pay for what they did."

She looked at Doug again, seeing the questioning look on his face. "Yes, Doug, it's the same man."

"It was about ten months later on a beautiful spring day when I first met him. I was sitting outside enjoying the afternoon sun, just watching the people walk by when a tall, good-looking man sat on the bench next to me. He did not say a word at first; he only sat there quietly. I didn't know what to think or do. Should I fear this man, or wait to see if he needed assistance. After a few awkward moments, he finally spoke, and what he said almost knocked me off the bench. *I have your purse from New Orleans, and I wanted you to have it back. I'm sorry it took me so long to return it, but I've been busy.* When he turned and looked at me, I suddenly found myself lost in the most striking blue eyes I have ever seen, but what I found hidden behind those eyes was a mixture of both pain and rage. He reached into his pack, pulled out my purse, and handed it to me without saying another word. My hands were trembling so hard that I was sure I would drop it. He looked at me again and said in a soft voice, *You have no need to fear me.*"

A small laugh had escaped her lips before she continued, "I smiled at him and said, Fear you? My goodness, I think I love you! You stopped those terrible men from being able to hurt anyone else, and for that, I will be forever grateful. I told him if there was ever anything, I could do for him, all he had to do was ask, and I would make sure it was done."

Doug sat in silence, transfixed by the story being told, but not quite sure what to think.

Sally smiled and then continued, "We became quite close over the next few years. He would come and stay with me from time to time then vanish for a few weeks or even months. I would never ask him where he was going or what he did. I knew his work was important, and I was willing to help him. However, I could. On one of his visits, he asked if I would receive his personal mail, and keep his valuable documents in a safe place for him. I, of course, was thrilled that he trusted me, and I gladly accepted his request," she lowered her eyes, not wanting to look directly at Doug.

"You're in love with him, aren't you?" Doug asked.

Sally did not look up. She had never uttered the words in her heart to anyone, and she was not sure if she even knew how to put them into words. "I love Ted, but not in the way you mean. We were two souls searching to be understood, searching for someone we could confide in and know there would never be any judgment passed. We have a special relationship; it's one that goes beyond the physical. It's pure in form, and I treasure it every day. I would do anything for Ted."

Doug shook his head, not sure of what to do with this information. "Why did he want me to have this letter now?" Doug held his breath, not sure if he wanted to hear her answer.

"He's dying, Doug. The damn Vietnam War is finally going to get him. He knows I'm too old to fulfill his wishes, so he wanted someone he respected to do it for him. We have talked for hours about you, and he has watched you for quite some time now. He knows what you've been through and that you're a man of honor. It was Ted who suggested that I rent the apartment to you when you put in your application."

"You mean he's been here all along?" Doug could not believe what he was hearing.

"Yes, in fact, you've met him," she said with a smile on her lips.

"What? When did I meet him?" Doug searched his memory.

"It was right after you moved in. Do you remember when your bathroom faucet was leaking? He was the one that fixed it." She fought to hold back the laughter at the shocked look that suddenly appeared on Doug's face.

"That was Ted? I thought it was some homeless guy you paid a few bucks for doing handyman work for you!"

Doug sat up straight, looking into Sally's eyes. "You know you've been breaking the law all these years, don't you?"

Sally sat up straight and looked back into Doug's eyes, and calmly said, "I don't care about any laws I may have broken. Ted has never hurt anyone who truly did not deserve it, and he has saved more people from a horrible death than you will ever know. Maybe it's wrong to take the law into your own hands, but sometimes the law lets all of us down. You can't sit there and tell me the thought of doing the very same thing hasn't entered your mind before. Ted told me how he had learned of your wife and child's murders, and how the man who did it only received a twenty-year sentence. Are you going to tell me the wish to make sure the man who murdered them paid for it more permanently has never crossed your mind? I have a hard time believing that, Doug."

"Of course, it has, but I would never act on it! It's just not right to take the law into your own hands and damn it, Sally; it's not right to help someone do it either." Doug shook his head, not sure of how to process this information.

"He did pay for it, Doug. Ted saw to it," she held her breath waiting as Doug realized what she had said.

"What! What the hell are you saying, Sally?" Doug blurted out, as the meaning of her words sunk into his mind.

Doug had been notified a couple of months earlier how the man who had murdered Donna and Miranda was killed during a riot. Ted learned that after they had secured the cellblock, they had found him dead from a stab wound on the right side of his neck. "But how did Ted have anything to do with that?"

"Revenge can be a powerful tool, but arranging for someone else to get their justice is better than money. You see, life at times will offer us an opportunity we cannot pass up. There was a man on the same cellblock as the one who killed your family. He was in there for attempting to kill the man who had raped and murdered his wife. The rapist had beaten the rap with a fake alibi, so on the day he was released, the grieving husband beat him nearly to death. Ted befriended the husband and made a deal with him. Ted would handle the man who had raped and murdered his wife, and he would take care of the man who killed Donna and Miranda. It's funny the strange gifts that life sometimes offers, isn't it?" Sally softly laughed as she leaned back in her chair and waited for his response.

Doug sat dumbfounded, unsure of how to respond. He was thrilled when he had learned the man who had destroyed his life was dead.

Hell, how many times did I dream that I was the one who did it, but I never expected this development? He thought to himself.

"I don't understand...why would he do that? I...ah, I don't know what to say."

"He did it for you and for your family. He has watched you for a long time now, and he has seen the same sadness in you that he has felt in himself. To lose everyone you loved and cared about is a pain that never goes away. To lose those you care for at the hands of a murderer is a pain that turns into rage, and will burn inside of you until the day you die."

Doug had never told Sally of his family. One time she had asked him why he had never married, but he told her he was too busy with his work to find someone. She had decided not to push the subject with him, but then the day came when Ted told her what he had done to the man who had murdered Doug's family. She wanted to say more but knew it was not the proper time yet. Ted had told her the day would come when she would have to be the one to relay the news, but this was not the time.

"I don't understand why you're telling me this now. You said he is dying, and he wants me to handle things for him because he thinks of me as a man of honor. Sally, I can't get involved in this...it's just wrong...," Doug protested, but Sally cut him off.

"Doug, you have to do this for him, please! He told you earlier he only needed a couple of more days to finish. Please, let him finish his work. It's so important, I promise you," Sally pleaded.

"Finish his work, just what the hell is he up to now?" Doug felt frustration build up inside of him.

"I don't know for sure, but I do know that it will be good for the city. Please, Doug, he doesn't have much time left to do his work." Tears streamed down her cheeks.

Doug stood and then looked down at Sally with a look of fear in his eyes. "He's going to kill again, isn't he?"

"I don't know, Doug. All he said was it was important to stop them, and he had to do it soon," she wiped her tears.

"Damn it, what the hell have you gotten yourself into, Sally? I need to get going; I'm already late." He handed the paperwork back to her and turned toward the door.

"Doug, please try to understand. He's on your side. He only wants to help," her words floated on the air, as Doug closed the screen door behind him and walked to his car.

Chapter 25

On the way to the station, Doug received a call of a murder a couple of miles away from his location.

Oh, crap, please don't let it have been him, Doug groaned, as he turned his car toward the address.

While Doug drove up the street, he noticed a small group of people gathered around, crying. He parked his car and then walked up to the officers questioning the people in the crowd.

"What happened here?" Doug asked while looking down at a young man lying in a pool of blood on the sidewalk.

"It sounds like he pissed off the wrong guys. His mother said they came up to the house and demanded money; they said the boy owed them. She said she did not recognize them and told them to go away. Apparently, that was when her son ran out the side door, but they caught him, and well, you can see what happened next."

The officer looked down at the visible bullet hole in the back of the young man's head and shook his head. "From what the neighbors have told us, the son was running drugs for the gang and made the mistake of helping himself to some of the profits. I guess they decided to send a clear message to anyone else who might consider doing the same thing."

Doug was sad to see the dead kid lying there but relieved to know that it had nothing to do with Ted. "Yeah, they did send a clear message. Well, I guess I better get busy," he smiled and then walked over to the gathered group of family and neighbors.

***

Doug was glad to be back at the station. He hated interviewing grieving families and watch as they faced the truth of their dead loved one. He had seen it many times, and it always amazed him that no matter how deep in trouble their loved one was, they would always seem to be in denial.

Doug sat at his desk and worked on what appeared to be endless paperwork, but his mind kept wandering back to his earlier conversation with Sally.

Damn it, why didn't she tell me before today? However, he knew the answer as soon as the thought entered his mind.

"What was it, she said? It wasn't the right time yet," he whispered to himself while putting the last form into a folder and setting it in the basket on the corner of his desk.

"Hey, Doug, are you alright?" Detective Dave Stevens asked as he walked up to Doug's desk. "You look like you got a lot on your mind."

"As a matter of fact, I do, but I'm not quite sure what I need to do about it," Doug shook his head.

"Is there anything I can do to help?" Dave asked.

"No. This is something I need to work out myself."

"Hey, I understand. Sometimes we just need a good night's sleep to figure things out and get them in perspective," Dave smiled then he turned and walked away. "Have a good one. I'll see you tomorrow."

"You too, Dave, and tell Sharon hello for me, okay?" Doug prayed this would end the conversation because he was not in the mood to talk.

"I will. You do remember that she still wants you to come over for dinner sometime?" Dave laughed.

"I know, she wants to introduce me to her co-worker," Doug grinned, trying to hide his discomfort at the idea.

"Come on, you can't stay single forever, and besides, she's a great gal," Dave laughed.

"I'm sure she is, but I'm not interested in meeting anyone," Doug muttered.

"Okay, maybe some other time." David realized there was no sense in pushing the subject anymore, so he turned and walked away.

Once Doug had finished all of the paperwork on his desk, he decided to go home and do some thinking about everything he had learned that day. He knew he should talk more with Sally, but he was not ready to learn anything more about Ted.

All he wanted was a hot shower and a good night's sleep. "Damn, I need to clear my mind of all of this, and get some rest," he groaned, as he walked outside to his car.

Doug pulled into his space at the apartment building, and while walking toward his apartment, he heard a familiar voice from the shadows. "Hello, handsome."

"Sugar, is that you?" Doug was surprised that Sugar would be the one calling to him. "When did you get out of the hospital?"

"They let me out today, Sweetie. I just couldn't wait to get out of there either. They were nice and all, but they didn't understand an ebony enchantress like me. Besides, poor Juliet was lost without me at home." Sugar laughed, brushing the hair from his eyes.

"Well, it's good to have you home and looking like yourself again. You sure gave us all quite a scare," Doug smiled.

He had to admit that he had always found the two of them to be quite amusing.

"Doug, I heard what happened to that horrible man who attacked us. I know you will probably not agree with me, but I'm glad. He was a cruel person who didn't care who he hurt," Sugar said with a touch of anger in his voice.

"Hey, what's going on out here? Oh, good evening, Doug. Would you like some tea?" Juliet asked while he walked to the bench where Sugar was sitting.

"No, thank you, Juliet. I was just welcoming Sugar home. I need to get some rest; it's been a long day," Doug stepped back to let Juliet pass by him, and then sit next to Sugar.

"Thank you for helping us that horrible night; we owe you a debt of gratitude," Sugar smiled, taking the cup of tea from Juliet.

"Hey, I'm just glad I was there to help, but more importantly, I'm relieved that you are doing fine and sitting here enjoying the evening," he smiled.

"Doug…," Juliet began to speak, but then changed his mind.

"What Juliet? Is there something you want to say?"

Sugar and Juliet exchanged worried looks before Sugar finally spoke, "Doug, we know who punished that horrible man." Sugar stopped long enough to see the look of surprise on Doug's face.

"He came to visit me at the hospital to let me know I would be safe, and the man who had attacked me would never be able to do it again. Please don't go after him, he's a good man, and he only wants to help."

The response from Doug surprised them both, "I know who he is as well. He's a friend of Miss Sally's, and his name is Ted Braxton."

"How do you know?" Juliet asked as he placed his cup of tea on the table beside the bench.

"I just found out today, but I haven't had the chance to grasp it fully. I need some rest, so I'll just bid you ladies' goodnight," Doug grinned, hoping to find a quick escape from this uncomfortable conversation.

"Goodnight and sweet dreams," Juliet and Sugar cooed.

Sugar looked at Juliet, as he watched Doug walk away, "He still is one fine-looking man, isn't he?"

"He sure is, honey. Would you like some more tea?" Juliet laughed as he picked up the pitcher to refill their cups.

***

Doug was glad to be in his apartment and away from the world. He had taken a long, hot shower hoping it would wash away the questions he had about the discoveries of the day.

He was relaxing in his recliner when his cell phone began to ring. "Damn it, who would be calling now?" Doug reached for his cell phone, "Hello."

"Hello, Doug, it's Ted. I understand that you've had a rather difficult day. I'm sorry to have dropped all this on you the way I did, but I'm running out of time. I know Sally told you how we met, and I'm hoping that you won't hold any of this against her. She's an incredible woman, and I'm grateful to have her in my life," Ted's voice was quiet and full of hope.

Doug paused, trying to think of the best response before he spoke. "You know you've made her a party to your crimes by her knowledge of them, and not reporting them to the authorities, don't you?" Doug hated the conflict growing inside of him, but he knew he must fight the urge for revenge. He knew he must be faithful to his values and the belief that it was wrong to take the law into your own hands, no matter how you felt.

Ted paused and then spoke with a deep sadness in his voice that surprised Doug. "I know you're right, and I never meant for it to happen that way. I would never do anything to hurt Sally. She's the only one who cares if I live or die," Ted's voice broke with the realization that without Sally, he was utterly alone.

"Doug, as a man realizes his life is coming to an end, he begins to evaluate what he will leave behind. I never married nor had any children, so my only legacy is that I was able to rid this great country of some evil people. I never hurt anyone who did not deserve it. I only wanted to make sure the victims of heinous crimes had a sense of peace with the knowledge that they finally received justice for the deeds committed against them. I had hoped you would understand. You've known the same pain of losing your family at the hands of a man that valued money over the lives of your wife and child…."

Doug could take it no longer. "Stop it! Stop talking about Donna and Miranda! Yes, I wanted that asshole dead! He took everything from me and for what, a few dollars? I had to come home to an empty house, and the first time I ever touched my daughter was while she was lying on a cold, metal table in the morgue. Their deaths are what drove me into law enforcement."

The emotions flowing from Doug were overwhelming. He hated the fact that deep in his heart, he envied the path Ted had chosen. He could not begin to count the number of times he had dreamed of ending the life of the man who had destroyed his family. Then to learn the truth of his demise had caused a conflict inside of Doug that he did not enjoy. "Having him killed was wrong! He should have…he should have died…"

Ted cut in. "He should have died by your hands?"

"Yes, damn it! It should have been me that ended his sorry life! I've dreamed thousands of times of looking him in the eyes as he realized that he was about to die. I wanted to be the one to send him to Hell…not…oh, God!" The rage and pain were more than Doug could handle.

Ted sensed that Doug's emotions were nearing the breaking point. "Doug, he died with the full knowledge of why. He knew his death was payment for the lives of a beautiful young mother and her sweet, baby daughter and that he would spend eternity paying for his evil deeds. He knew Doug. He knew, and he suffered as he lay dying on that cold prison floor."

Hearing the words brought Doug to the breaking point. Tears streamed down his face, and he felt something new overtake him: Peace.

For the first time in years, he did not feel the rage burning deep in his soul. "I know I shouldn't say this, but thank you. I want to thank you for making him suffer for what he did to them," Doug cried, wiping the tears from his face.

There was a long silence before Ted spoke, "You're welcome. I hope it lets you find some peace. I know it's late, and you need to rest, so I'll let you go for now. I hope you'll think about my request, but if you choose not to do it, I'll understand."

Doug did not know what to say. He had not thought about the request all day. With everything else going on it, had completely slipped his mind.

"Ted, can you tell me what you meant when you said you had one last thing to do?" Doug knew he probably would not get an answer, but he had to try.

"I wish I could because you have a critical role in it. I'll tell you at the proper time but now is not that time. You need your rest, so we'll talk again soon. Goodnight, Doug."

Doug knew there was no sense asking again, so he would just have to wait. "Goodnight and I look forward to the next time we talk." They both hung up.

Doug sat, not sure, of what to think of the things Ted had told him. "I have a critical role in his plan? What the hell does he mean by that?" Doug wondered aloud.

"I can't get involved in what he does," but no sooner had the words left his mouth; he knew they were a lie. He was involved from the moment he did not report the first time he had spoken with Ted and learned the truth.

Why didn't I say something? The question burned in his mind, but he knew the truth. Ted was the part of himself that he had kept buried all these years.

Doug knew his feelings were wrong, but he could not help himself, and besides, Ted was dying, so why arrest him now.

"Damn it, I know what I need to do. I need to leave my personal feelings out of this and just do my job!" The frustration churned inside of Doug. He knew what he should do, but was it what he wanted to do? He looked at the clock and realized it was late.

"Crap! I need to get to bed." Doug walked to his bedroom, but he knew he would never sleep with everything on his mind.

Chapter 26

The sound of the alarm brought Doug out of a deep, fitful sleep. He had no idea what time he had finally drifted off to sleep, but he knew it was late.

"Shit, why did all of this have to happen now?" Doug growled as he got out of bed and walked to the bathroom.

"Maybe a shower will help." He pulled the shower curtain back and stepped in.

The warm water felt good, as Doug pondered the current events with a growing sense of dread. Doug knew he should take Miss Sally and Sugar in for questioning, but he could not bring himself to do it.

There has to be a way to keep them out of this! The thought screamed in his mind, but how would he do it?

Doug knew he was wrong to withhold evidence, but he could not bring himself to involve them.

"Damn it!" Doug groaned as he got out of the shower. He knew he must decide soon, but for the life of him, he did not have a clue as to what to do. Part of him knew what was right, but the other part knew what he wanted.

After he had dressed, he decided to leave early for work. As he opened his front door to leave, he prayed Sally was still asleep because he was not in the mood to talk to her just yet.

***

Doug was thankful that he had only paperwork to do this morning. Over the years, he found the tedious chore to be the perfect distraction from whatever was bothering him at the time, but today it did not seem to do the trick.

What am I going to do? He thought to himself.

He knew what he should do, but he could not bring himself to do it. There had to be a way to stop Ted and keep Sally out of it. The problem was, did he want to stop Ted before he finished his work?

"Damn it! I need to get out of here and clear my head," Doug growled as he put the paperwork back into their folders.

Doug decided a good way to take his mind off Ted was to question the mother of the slain boy. He hoped that she might have additional information about the gang and her son's involvement with them.

***

"My son was a good boy until he hooked up with those street thugs," Clarise Wilson cried, as she held a picture of her son against her breast. "He changed, though. He wasn't the same sweet boy."

The tears streamed down her face, and Doug thought to himself of how much older she looked today. "Mrs. Wilson, I'm sorry for your loss, but I need any additional information you may have to help me find your son's killer. However, the words she said next shocked Doug.

"Don't worry, Detective; my boy will get his justice. I know this because a man promised me that he would," Clarise said with a newfound strength.

"He told me the people who did that to my son would meet their fate, and they would no longer be able to destroy the lives of the young men in the neighborhood."

Doug tried to think of what to say next. *Ted said he had one last thing to do, and it would be good for the city. Damn, they must be his next target!* The words screamed in his mind.

"Are you feeling alright, Detective? You look flushed," Clarise said, noticing his expression. "Do you need a drink of water?"

"No, thank you, I'm okay. May I ask when you talked to this man, and can you tell me what he looked like?" Doug took a deep breath, trying to compose himself.

"Well, let's see. He looked to be about sixty years old, six feet tall, and with the most striking blue eyes I've ever seen." She stopped once she saw the shocked look on Doug's face. "Are you sure you're alright, Detective? You don't look so well."

"Yes, I'm fine. You said he had blue eyes. Do you remember anything else about him?" Doug held his breath and waited.

Clarise sat back and thought a moment. "He was soft-spoken and with a slight southern drawl. I didn't know what to think of him at first, but he said my son's death would not be in vain. He said that I would find peace in the knowledge that those who had killed him would pay for what they had done."

A smile crossed her face as she continued, "I know my son chose the wrong path, but he didn't deserve to die like that. They shot him like you would a mad dog and for what; the few dollars he took from them. I hope that man keeps his promise and makes them pay!" She looked at Doug and smiled.

Doug sat there, not sure how to respond to her. "Mrs. Wilson, I know you want justice for your son, but that isn't the way. A vigilante dispensing justice is not allowed by our laws. If you can just be patient...," but Clarise cut him off.

"Be patient? My neighbor is still awaiting justice for the murder of her six-year-old daughter! The sweet little thing was just playing in her bedroom when a bullet came through the window and killed her. No one in that house had anything to do with the gangs around here, so the police told us they must have hit the house by mistake. By mistake? There was no mistake watching that sweet, little girl being put in the ground, or seeing the fear on the faces of the children who live in this neighborhood. If that man can get justice for the death of my boy, then I wish him success, and if that makes me a bad person, then so be it! I know someday I will go meet my maker, and if he thinks I was wrong for feeling the way I do then I'll answer to him, but there is nothing you can say to change how I feel." She closed her eyes and leaned back in her chair.

Doug knew there was nothing more he could say. "Mrs. Wilson, I'm sorry for your loss, and I promise to do everything I can to find who killed your son. If you hear from the man again, or if you remember anything more, would you please contact me? Here's my card with the number at the station, as well as the number for my cell phone. Please take care of yourself, and thank you for your time; I'll let myself out."

He knew she would not call if she heard from Ted again, but he had to try.

Doug stood and walked to the door, but he stopped when he heard Clarise speak again. "Detective, you seem like a nice man, and I'm sure you're just as tired of those people as we are. If the man says he can take care of them, why do you need to stop him? I know the good book says *Vengeance is mine saith the Lord*, but I also believe the Lord provides us with a soldier to do his bidding from time to time." She said with a soft smile on her lips.

The words cut into Doug with such force that no response came to his mind. "Thank you again for your time," was the only thing he could think to say as he walked out of the door.

The drive back to the station was difficult for Doug. He knew in his mind, he must do everything to stop Ted, but his heart agreed with Mrs. Wilson.

"Damn it, you know what you need to do. Now do it!" he chastised himself as he pulled into his parking space at the station.

He then grabbed the ignition key to turn off the car when his cell phone rang. "Hello, this is Detective Mabry." Doug had hoped it was Mrs. Wilson with additional information; however, it was not her.

"Hello, Doug. I hope your day is going well?" Ted asked.

"It could be better. I just had a visit with Mrs. Wilson, and she informed me that the two of you have met. Damn it, what are you up to?" Frustration was evident in his voice.

Ted paused a moment before answering, "Doug, you know that I only have one more job to do, correct? I've been watching them for a while now, and I can assure you that they are responsible for several murders in the area, as well as selling drugs to the children in the neighborhood. I know the police have worked hard to solve the cases, but the people in the community are too frightened to help. I'm not bound by the same limitations, as you are Doug. You see, I'm free to be a bit creative. I respect the law, but I also understand when someone uses the law against us. Tonight, they will pay for their evil deeds."

Doug could not believe what he was hearing. "Ted, you can't...please, don't do this!"

Doug pleaded, but he knew his words were empty, as he also found himself thrilled at the news.

"It's already set in motion, so there is no going back now. I promise no harm will come to the innocent, but as for those involved, their deaths will be filled with both terror and pain. I need to go; I still have a few last-minute things to do. I'll contact you once everything is done." Ted did not wait for a response because he knew Doug would try to stop him.

"Ted, please...wait...," but his pleas went unheard. Doug sat in his car, questioning what he should do. He knew he should call for an all-out search, but where? Besides, he did not want to explain why he failed to report this sooner.

He knew he was treading on dangerous ground with keeping this a secret, but a voice deep inside of him kept telling him to hold tight, and that all would work out.

Suddenly a thought came to him. *Sally, I need to talk to Sally!*

The words screamed in his mind, as he put the still-running car in reverse and backed out of his space.

"Sally will know what he's planning to do!" he said aloud as he pulled out of the parking lot and rushed back to his apartment.

Chapter 27

As Doug walked up the sidewalk, he heard music and laughter coming from Sally's apartment.

Good, she's home, he thought to himself.

Doug had hoped she would be alone, but he knew he could not wait until her guests left. He needed to talk to her now, so with determination, he knocked on her screen door.

"One minute," a little voice came from the guest bedroom.

"It's Doug, may I come in?" he asked impatiently.

"Oh, yes, come on in dear. Please give me just a moment," she replied, as Doug heard deep giggles come from the room.

"Sugar and Juliet are here, and we're enjoying some dress-up time." This statement now brought loud giggles from the room.

At hearing this, Doug wished that he had not come, as the mental picture appearing in his mind was something that he could have lived the rest of his life without seeing.

"Ah…no problem, I'll just sit and wait…ah…take your time," Doug said, feeling the warmth move up his neck and across his face.

Sally appeared from the guest room in one of the most unusual costumes Doug had ever seen. It was a long, tight-fitting dress with what looked like feathers around the neck, waist, and flowing down behind the dress, like a peacock's tail.

She carried an even stranger looking hat in her hands, covered in feathers and strung jewels. "Oh, Dougie, it's always a pleasure to see you. What brings you by this time of the day?" She placed the hat on the table beside her chair, and then she undid the clasp holding the feathered tail and laid it on the floor next to the table. Finally, she sat in her chair and looked over at Doug.

"I'm not sure where to start. I received a call from Ted, and he said that later today, he would be making his final move on the gang responsible for the murder of that young man the other day. Do you know anything about this?" He held his breath and waited.

Sally smiled and said in a soft voice. "I knew the time was coming for him to do his final act, but I didn't know who his target was.

Doug, you must understand something, Ted would never tell me the details of what he had planned because he would not want to burden me with the knowledge of that information. I would hear from time to time what he had done, but, for the most part, I never knew, or even wanted to know. I'm sorry, but I can't help you."

Doug looked deeply into her eyes, trying to see if she was honest with him. He knew that she cared for Ted and would probably lie for him, but for some reason, he believed that she was telling him the truth.

"Okay, Sally, I was just hoping you would help me stop Ted before he fulfilled his plan." Doug hated the feelings churning inside of him. First, he was angry with Ted for involving him, but, for the most part, now he was disappointed for not being in on the final plan to bring down the gang.

"Why would I want to stop Ted? He has helped so many people over the years, and I would never come between him and his mission in life. Soon he will be gone, and the world will be a better place because of his having been here. I know you have a job to do, so go do it. I respect what you do, but remember that Ted has a job to do as well.

We as a society have all benefited from what he does," Sally leaned toward Doug with tears streaming down her face. "If you feel the need to arrest me, then so be it. I will proudly go to jail and face whatever punishment you have for me!"

Doug realized his visit was a waste of time. "I'm sorry for upsetting you. I just thought you might know what was going to happen. I'll leave you to your festivities. Goodbye, Sally... goodbye, Sugar and Juliet," Doug stood and walked to the door. "If you change your mind, you know how to reach me."

"Goodbye, Doug," Sugar and Juliet said from the guest room.

"Goodbye, Dougie, we'll talk again later," Sally said with a hint of sadness in her voice.

***

Doug decided to grab a bite to eat, so he went across the walkway to his apartment.

"Damn it, there has to be a way to figure out what he's going to do!" Doug growled as he opened the refrigerator. He grabbed the lunchmeat and mayonnaise jar and set them on the counter. He was about to open the bread package when his cell phone rang. "Hello, this is Detective Mabry."

"Doug, this is Ted. You may want to call your department, and report multiple homicides," his voice was strained, but calm.

"Oh, my God, you've done it, haven't you?" Doug felt a chill flow over him.

"Let us just say that they will no longer be able to hurt anyone," Ted paused a moment to catch his breath.

"Do you remember the building where the two drug runners were killed a few months back? You need to go to apartment 203 because I have left you a mess that needs to be cleaned up." Ted coughed, and then continued, "I must be getting slow, Doug. One of the bastards was able to get a hold of his gun and got a shot off. Well, it didn't go too well for him after that. Nothing pisses me off more than to get shot," he chuckled.

"There are fourteen bodies in the apartment, and one in the entry hall. Most people will believe it was a hit from a rival gang, but you'll know the truth. It's your choice to decide what you want to do with this information," Ted coughed again, this time causing his voice to become raspy and weak.

Doug did not know what to think. How should he handle this information? Should he let everyone believe it was a hit by a rival gang, or should he tell the truth?

The truth, how could he explain that he had known for some time the identity of the vigilante was, but never reported it?

I'm screwed, no matter what I do! Doug thought to himself.

"Ted, you've put me in a difficult place. How can I explain that I know about the killings without involving you? Damn you!" The emotions surged through Doug, as he realized the choice he had to make.

"Doug, I have faith in you. You're an honorable man and will do what your heart says is right. I count myself privileged to have been able to get to know you. I need to go now. Please remember my request, Doug," the call ended.

"Shit!" Doug had hoped to learn where Ted was, but he knew it was hopeless to look for him. Doug put the lunchmeat and mayonnaise back into the refrigerator and then headed outside to his car.

Once he was in his car, an announcement came over his radio with the same address that Ted had given to him. As Doug pulled out of the driveway, he wondered what mayhem Ted had left behind for him to clean up.

***

When Doug pulled up to the building, he noticed several patrol cars parked out front, and two officers questioning a small group of residents. He got out of his car and walked up to the group, but what he heard from one of the residents surprised him.

"It was terrible, Officer! There were around ten of them, and they charged in the building and upstairs to the apartment where the drug dealers lived. We heard them break in the door, and then the shooting and screaming began. We knew it was a hit from another gang, so we all just stayed in our apartments and waited until they left," the young woman said, as the others nodded in agreement.

What is she saying? Doug stood there dumbfounded by what he was hearing.

He walked closer to the group when the officer questioning her had noticed him. "Detective Mabry, I'm glad you're here. This looks to be the result of a rival gang. There are bodies all over the place up there. It's a hell of a mess. I don't think I'll ever get that vision out of my mind." A shiver moved over him again at the memory of what happened to the victims.

"All I can say is they must have really pissed off the other gang for them to have done some of the things they did."

Doug had watched the young woman the entire time the officer was speaking, and what he read on her face surprised him. He did not see fear there; instead, he saw joy. She tried to act upset by all the events, but her eyes betrayed her true feelings.

Once she realized Doug was watching her, she turned to meet his gaze, and then gave him a slight smile, and a wink.

What the hell? She's lying! She's making this whole story up to cover for Ted! The words screamed in his mind at the idea of someone else involved in the cover-up.

"Are you alright, Detective?" the young woman asked Doug, as a new look of concern crossed her face.

Doug composed himself and answered, "Yes, I'm good."

He then turned to the other officer and said, "I'm going to see for myself. It looks like you have everything handled here for now." Doug needed to get away from this uncomfortable situation.

What did Ted do for you to make you lie for him, young lady? Doug turned and walked toward the entryway of the building while wondering what he would find upstairs.

***

The scene laid out before Doug was worse than he could have ever imagined. As he walked up to the door of the apartment, he noticed a body lying in the hallway. He looked down and saw a large, gaping wound in the throat of the victim, but what struck Doug as strange was how he had been shot in both eyes. It also surprised him how they found the body as if staged that way.

You must be the one who shot Ted, Doug snickered as he looked down at the body while trying to find a gun.

"Hey, did any of you find a gun on or near this body?" Doug asked, but he knew the answer before anyone could answer.

"No, sir, this one was unarmed. He must have been trying to get away because he was the only one that we found out here," the officer said as he walked over to Doug. "Shit, I've never been called out to anything like this before. It looks like a damn war zone in there."

Doug did not respond; he only turned and walked inside the apartment, but nothing could have prepared him for the scene that awaited him. Blood was splattered everywhere. It was all over the floors, the walls, and even on the ceiling. There were bodies strewn about the room, and it appeared that several of them had no time to react before they were slaughtered.

Several seemed to have been trying to escape but were unable to before they met their fate.

What was it that Ted had said? They would die knowing terror and pain. Doug hated how this made him feel. To know someone like Ted was capable of doing something so dark and cruel, terrified Doug.

"It looks like this one is going to take a while to clean up. I sure am glad that I'm not on the Homicide Investigative Team for this one," the officer standing next to the window said with a nervous laugh.

"Yeah, it's a hell of a mess, isn't it?" Doug chuckled while trying to hide his real feelings. "I think I'll go back down and question the witnesses before the media has a chance to get a hold of them.

***

It was late into the night before Doug was able to go home. He was tired and angry.

Why did Ted involve me in all this, and why did I allow him to do it?

The thought burned in his mind as he pulled into his parking space at home and turned off his car. He got out of his car and was walking toward his apartment when he heard crying coming from the bench under the tree where he had spoken with Sugar and Juliet.

"What the hell." He walked toward the sound. "Who's there?"

"Hello, Doug." Ted was sitting on the bench, clutching his stomach with Sally sitting next to him, attempting to hold him in place. Doug could see the blood soaking through his shirt and on his hand.

"I told you I must be getting slow, but I showed him, didn't I?" Ted laughed, but the pain was evident on his face.

"I want to let you know they will never find the gun that asshole shot me with, so I can never be tied to the killings." Ted grimaced again as another wave of pain shot through his body.

"Why would you worry about protecting your name now, Ted? You've left a wave of carnage in your path, and…"

Sally cut Doug off mid-sentence. "Shut up, Doug. You have no idea what you're talking about," Sally snarled. "He has done a lot for this community, for what?"

Ted reached out and took Sally's hand in his. "It's alright; he doesn't understand. Doug, I was seen when I was leaving. A young woman I had saved a few months ago from being raped by a group of street thugs saw me. She recognized me and told me she would make sure the police would have a story to lead them in the wrong direction. I can tell by the look on your face that she must have kept her promise. Doug, I couldn't have her get into trouble for giving a false report by letting myself be tied to the case." Ted grimaced again, as a more powerful wave of pain shot through his body.

"Doug, I don't have much time left. I want you to promise me that you won't punish Sally for my actions. She has never hurt anyone, and she deserves to live the rest of her life here, and in peace. I'm sorry we never got to know each other better. I do think if life was different, we could have been great friends," Ted coughed, and Doug noticed blood now spreading across his lips.

"You need to be in the hospital, Ted," Doug frowned as he reached for his cell phone and began to dial.

"No, don't call. I don't want to go to the hospital. I want to stay here and enjoy the beautiful night. I want this to be the last thing I see, not some cold hospital room."

Ted's hand tightened on Sally's, as their eyes locked together. "Thank you for always being there for me. You've been my one true friend, and I want you to know that I have treasured our time together."

Sally's heart was breaking. She smiled and kissed his hand. "You will always be in my heart, Ted," she cried as the tears flowed down her cheeks.

Those were the last words Ted heard, as he took his final breath.

Doug looked down at the still body. "Goodbye, Ted, I will remember to protect your honor."

***

"Yes, officer, she's my landlord, and she is quite shaken up by the whole thing. She said she heard a strange noise, and came outside to see what it was. She found him sitting on the bench, holding his stomach, and covered in blood. Before he died, he told her that he was shot in a robbery attempt a few blocks away and somehow made it here looking for help. He was an acquaintance of hers, and she had hired him from time to time to do work for her," Doug explained, hoping the story would suffice.

"Thank you, Detective Mabry, for your help. I'm sure you know as well as I do the chance of catching the perpetrator is slim," the officer said, as he moved out of the way for the coroner to gather up his equipment.

"At least someone knows who he is, so he won't end up being just another John Doe."

"Yeah, no one deserves to die and not have anyone left behind to remember what you've done with your life. Everyone is worthy of a legacy and most especially if you served your country with honor," Doug said, remembering Ted's request.

Epilogue

Four Years Later

"Oh, Doug, this is such a beautiful place, but I'm glad we're almost there because this has been a long trip," Cindy Mabry laughed as she looked over at Doug.

It was a beautiful fall day in Southeast Texas. Doug had decided to bring his family to the birthplace and final resting place of the man who had changed his life forever. "Yes, this is it; there is our turn just up ahead."

Doug turned down the road and followed it for about three miles to the entrance of the cemetery. He felt his heart pound in his chest, as they turned in the gate, and he was surprised at the feeling of excitement growing inside of him.

"Are you okay?" Cindy asked.

"Yeah, I'm okay. I'm just remembering the man we're going to visit and introduce to our son," Doug smiled as he pulled into a parking space and turned off the car.

"Come on, you two, I have someone I'm anxious for you to meet."

They walked through the rows of headstones until they came to a group of four, all with the name Braxton on them. Doug stood there and read each one carefully. There was one for his father, one for his mother and a baby girl, and one for his brother. Then he turned to his wife and pointed to the one on the right that said:

Theodore James Braxton
A Great man and Marine
He served his country with honor

"Sweetheart, I want you to meet Ted Braxton. I owe him so much. He taught me that life is a gift and not to be wasted. He also taught me never to hide from life's gifts as well. For far too many years I was doing just that; I was hiding from my life," Doug said, taking her hand in his.

"Ted, I'm sorry it took me so long to come for a visit. I've been a bit busy as I'm sure you can see. I want you to know that I now have a beautiful family to ensure my legacy."

Doug's voice cracked as he continued, "I would like you to meet my lovely wife, Cindy, and our son, Justin Theodore Mabry. We named him after Cindy's grandfather, but I hope you do not mind us giving him your name as well. I thought it was the least I could do since it was because of you that I have my family." Doug smiled as he looked down at the grave with a single tear flowing down his cheek.

"We brought your mother and little sister some flowers for their grave, I hope they like them."

Doug set his son down, and Cindy gave him the flowers they had brought with them. She then guided him over to Mrs. Braxton's grave and had him rest the flowers against the headstone. Once they were in place, she picked him up and stepped back to stand beside Doug.

"Ted, I'm glad to have had the honor of knowing you. Even though we didn't agree on many things, I did learn a critical lesson from you, and for that, I will be eternally grateful. Thank you for showing me how not to let my life pass me by and how sometimes two wrongs can, in fact, make a right."

He looked one last time at the headstone, stood straight, and gave a sharp salute.

"Rest well, my brother in arms; I pray you have found eternal peace." With those words,

Doug turned and walked back to the car with Cindy and their son by his side.

A Message from the Author

I wish to thank you for taking the time to read Pure Justice, and I would like to invite you to read my other books.

Please take a moment to leave a review